A Hug Can Heal A Thousand Hearts

BY MERRILL OSMOND AND SHIRLEY BAHLMANN

Chapter 1

Catriona headed for the door, already wearing her new batwing sunglasses with glittering rhinestones. She took hold of the doorknob and turned, her brown curls swaying as she called, "Come on, Quigley!" Squinting in the dim indoor light, she spied her dog sitting next to Gran's chair, watching Catriona with anxious eyes. Strange. He was always eager to go out. "Come on," Catriona said, rolling one hand toward herself. "We're going to see Officer Lamb."

Quigley raised his furry eyebrows to look up at Gran with pleading brown eyes. Gran set aside her romance novel long enough to rub Quigley's funny ears sticking out on either side of his head. Instead of closing his eyes to soak up the attention as he usually did, he kept watching her.

"Maybe he's sick," Gran said, leaning forward to cup her hand beneath Quigley's chin and lift his lip, exposing sharp canine teeth.

"What are you doing?" Catriona abandoned the doorknob, lifted her sunglasses to the top of her head, and walked over to her grandmother. "You're not an animal doctor," she said with a fond smile.

Gran let go of Quigley but kept her elbows on her knees, studying him. "I thought I might see if his gums were pale or something."

Catriona sighed and rubbed a hand lightly across her Gran's back in a slow circle. "You just like to help everyone, don't you?"

Gran sighed and closed her eyes. "That feels good. Helping others feels good, too."

"Well, you're right good at it." Catriona used both hands to trace circles on Gran's back. Gran was the only mother she had, since Cat couldn't even remember Linnea, who'd given birth to her thirteen years ago. Gran assured her that Linnea had been a good mum as long as her husband was alive. It was only after four-year-old Catriona solemnly pronounced, "Daddy dead," just one day before her father's fatal traffic accident that Linnea saw her daughter differently. No longer an innocent child, Cat was blamed as the tool for her father's death, so Linnea abandoned her to Gran's care, and left their lives for good. Sometimes Cat wondered if Gran even knew where Linnea was.

Last night, she overheard Gran talking on the phone again to someone named Marlow. Gran didn't speak to Marlow often, the calls conducted quietly after Catriona was in bed. But she knew in the way she could feel things about people close to her, sensing Gran's emotions while on the phone with the mysterious Marlow - the tension, the yearning, the love. But since Gran never mentioned Marlow's name, Cat never asked who it was.

Last night, the call was different. Gran's side of the conversation was more heated than Cat had ever heard before. "You will not use her that way, Marlow," Gran said. "I will not have her suffer as she did with Linnea." There was a pause before Gran said with a distinct quaver in her voice, "Why can't you leave it in God's hands?"

A wave of despair rolled off of Gran, through the door, and over Cat so strongly that she pulled a pillow over her head to try to block it out. She loved Grandma Tilly Reid so much, from her thick toenails painted pastel violet or butter yellow to her softly wrinkled skin and hair dyed a warm chestnut, that it was hard to feel her distress.

Even though Gran didn't really understand why Catriona was different from other children, to her credit, she never told her to try fitting in. She simply accepted her granddaughter, visions and all. When Cat told Gran a few months ago that something frightening was coming, but she didn't know what it was, Gran gave her a helpless look. "I don't know how to sort that, love."

So Cat tried telling the police. They hadn't believed her until a young man from Hawaii named Liam helped Catriona connect with Officer Lamb. Once Officer Lamb understood that she wasn't just making things up, he became her ally.

Cat hoped she'd grow out of seeing events and feeling others' emotions, but so far, things she didn't ask for still brushed her mind and sometimes barged right in.

When Cat stopped rubbing Gran's back, Gran twisted around, caught one of Catriona's hands, and kissed it. Then she let go and leaned against the back of her chair. "Can you see anything wrong with him?"

Cat knelt down beside Quigley and petted his head. She'd only had him for a few months, ever since Liam was knocked unconscious at a Stonehenge riot and woke up on the Eurotrain bound for France. Even though he wasn't in England anymore, there were times when Catriona could visit Liam in her dreams.

As Catriona focused on Quigley's eyes, she felt a wave of incredible sadness. "He's sad," she said, her voice soft with surprise.

"About what?"

"I don't see everything, Gran," Catriona reminded her, "only some things, and they don't always make sense."

Gran reached out and pet Quigley again. "Poor boy. Can you tell if he's sad because you might get hurt if you go out?"

Catriona's gaze wandered over Quigley's short golden fur standing up in criss cross scars from his abuse as a puppy. "What is it?" she whispered to him. "What's wrong?"

Quigley's eyes shone as he looked at her, then he glanced back at Gran just as she sneezed.

"Bless you," Cat said. Then she asked, "Is it Gran?"

"It can't be me," Gran said. "I feel fine."

Quigley whined.

Catriona asked Quigley, "Do you miss Liam?"

Gran's brow furrowed. "Where is that boy again?"

"In a valley hidden from the world."

"Is he hiding from the law?"

"No, too much publicity. The whole world was after him for his predictions."

Catriona knew in the way she hated, because it was different from anyone else, the way she just knew things sometimes, that Quigley wasn't sad because he missed Liam. The dog was perfectly happy with Catriona.

Cat finally sighed and stood up. "Come on then, Quigley, you'll feel better after a walk."

Quigley resolutely nuzzled Gran's shoulder. Gran gave his neck a swift rub, then picked up her book. "If you're sad that I'm not going with you, then you'll just have to be sad, my boy. I didn't sleep well last night, and I've got a raging good novel to finish. I'll see you both for lunch."

Cat pulled her sparkly new glasses back down onto her nose, took hold of Quigley's collar, and pulled him to the door. The dog didn't take his eyes off Gran until the door closed. Then he sighed and trudged along behind Cat to the police station.

Cat waited just long enough for Quigley to squeeze through the station door behind her, then let the door close with a bang, shutting them in with the faint smells of paper, leather and gun cleaning oil. The officer at the desk looked up, a deep line between his brows until he saw Catriona. Then he touched his finger beside his eye and gave a nod before turning back to his computer screen.

Cat hesitated, unsure if his gesture was meant to indicate that she was daft or that he'd noticed her new eye wear. To bolster her courage, Catriona pushed her glasses firmly against the bridge of her nose. "Excuse me, is Officer Lamb in?"

The desk policeman jerked his head to one side without moving his eyes from the computer. Cat and Quigley strode down the hall to Officer Lamb's door, which was slightly ajar, letting out the voices inside. She stopped, but Quigley kept right on going, pushing his nose in the gap and forcing the door to swing wide. As soon as he cleared the door jamb, he scampered like a puppy, toenails clicking over the linoleum floor as he made his way to the young new sergeant, Charlie Walters, who sat across the desk from Officer Lamb. The sergeant's dark skin and shaved head contrasted with the officer's pale skin and graying hair.

"Sorry to interrupt," Catriona said from the doorway.

Lamb's eyes crinkled, indicating a smile beneath his mustache. "I hope you don't also prefer the sergeant to me, because it's obvious that Quigley does."

"No!" Catriona said, lifting her glasses up so that Officer Lamb couldn't miss the sincerity in her eyes. "You were the first kind one, my favorite bobby of them all."

"Good." He winked at Catriona. "I'm more of a cat person anyway. Now, then, what's that you've got on your head?"

Cat grinned, pulled her glasses off, and held them up. "New sunglasses."

Lamb whistled. "Fancy."

Cat looked at him, her face puzzled. "Are you alright?"

"As rain." The officer's eyebrows lifted. "Sorry if I can't whistle a proper tune."

"It wasn't your whistling," Catriona said, her eyes narrowing. "It's something… inside."

"Got me a bit of heartburn." Lamb patted his chest. "Shouldn't have had two helpings of fried potatoes at breakfast."

"True. You should have brought me some," Sergeant Walters said, scrubbing at Quigley's ears until they flapped around like demented bird's wings.

"I don't think he likes that," Catriona said, in spite of Quigley's closed eyes and blissful expression.

Walters stopped and pulled his hands away, his warm black eyes studying Cat's face. "If you say so." He rubbed his hand over his head while Quigley gave Catriona an accusing glance.

"He was very sad this morning," Cat explained.

"Why?" Lamb pulled open a desk drawer and rummaged inside.

Cat shrugged. "Maybe he didn't want to come here."

"Perhaps this will change his mind." Lamb tossed out half a stick of licorice so old it clattered to the floor. Quigley trotted over to it, sniffed, and picked it up in his jaws while settling to the floor to crunch on it.

"Sugar's not good for dogs," Walters said at the same time Catriona said, "He's not supposed to have that." Cat glanced at Walters in surprise. She didn't know him well, as he'd only been at the station for a month, but now she could almost forgive Quigley for favoring him.

"Oh, now, it hasn't hurt me any, has it?" Lamb tapped his round belly with the palm of his hand while the corners of his mustache turned up.

Catriona knelt to pull the licorice from Quigley's mouth, but he turned away.

"Here, boy!" Walters commanded as he bent down and held his hand beneath Quigley's nose. Quigley dropped what was left of the wet, mutilated licorice into the sergeant's hand. "Good boy! Now I think I have something for you in my pack that's good for dogs. Come along."

Although not as tall as Officer Lamb, Sergeant Walters' muscled arms crowded the doorway as he strode through it with Quigley at his heels.

"Just a minute." Catriona scrambled to her feet. "What are you giving him?"

"You'd better go see," Lamb said from his desk.

Cat took off out the door, trying to keep up. When the sergeant and her dog turned into the locker room, Cat hesitated at the door. A faint odor of sweat wafted toward her. Was this room just for officers? What if some male officer was in there taking a shower or walking around without anything on?

Suddenly, Quigley howled, a sound so forlorn that Catriona's heart jumped and her eyes filled with tears. Without another thought, she dashed into the room where Quigley sat on his haunches, muzzle lifted to the ceiling, the sergeant looking at him in bewilderment.

"What happened?" Cat asked, kneeling beside Quigley and throwing her arms around him.

Walters held his hands out at his sides. "I don't know. He was just following me and then suddenly started howling. I was only going to give him a piece of my sandwich. He can have tuna on wheat, can't he?"

"I think so. Yes. I don't know," Cat's answer came in gasps that accompanied Quigley's heart-rending howls. "I need to take him home."

"There's a door here." Walters hurried across the room and rammed into a push bar on a stout metal door marked "Emergency Exit." "It locks behind you, so you can't come back in this way."

"I'm not coming back today," Catriona said, pulling the now whimpering Quigley to the door by his collar. "Everything's too muddled."

"I'll tell John," Walters said. "Uh, that's Officer Lamb."

Cat didn't reply as she started down the road with her dog shuffling along beside her. Sergeant Walters watched them for a moment with troubled eyes before letting the door close behind them.

Chapter 2

Sergeant Walters found Officer Lamb fanning himself with a folded piece of paper. "Maybe you'd cool off a bit if you shaved that mustache," Charlie joked.

"This mustache is as much a part of me as my foot," John replied with a pained smile.

"You could live without it." Charlie rubbed a hand over his smooth head and down his shaven face.

"But then Catriona might not recognize me."

"She's not here anymore. She's taken Quigley home."

"What was all that howling about?"

Charlie shrugged "The dog just started in." He sat down. "You really like that girl, don't you?"

John leaned back, his face sweaty in the glare of the overhead light. "Yes, I do."

"She seems rather prickly to me."

"That's because her dog likes you, and she doesn't want to lose him."

Charlie scoffed. "I'd never take her dog from her, even though he's a winner." He tilted his head. "Just what is it you like about her?"

John closed his eyes. "A more honest person you could never hope to know. She's funny, sweet, and quirky. Do you remember that colorful hat with bells that she always used to wear?"

"Yeah. Haven't seen it lately, though."

John reached inside his desk and drew out a knitted cap as colorful as a balloon bouquet, with small bells that tinkled when he moved it.

"How did you get it?"

"She gave it to me for safekeeping."

"Why? Who'd ever want to nick a thing like that? A clown?"

"She wore it to try and block her visions, but decided to have a go without it."

"She's a strange duck."

John's eyes flew open, and his eyebrows took a dangerous dive. "How do you mean that?"

"No offense. It's just the way she looks at you, it's like she sees right through you. For example, how'd she know you had heartburn?"

"I told her."

"She seemed to know before you said anything."

"Neither of us knows what she was thinking."

Charlie leaned forward. "That's the problem. I feel like she knows what I'm thinking."

John gave a grudging grin. "Then you'd better only think things you want her to know."

Charlie rounded his shoulders. "That's a tall order."

"Just treat her like a normal girl, unless she comes to you with troubling tales of future events."

"Do you think she really knows what's going to happen?"

John rubbed a hand over his chest. "I do. At least some things." He grimaced. "Be a pal, will you, and get me some bicarbonate?"

"I'll see what I can find." Charlie headed for the door, then turned. "Why don't you take the rest of the day off?"

"You sure?"

Charlie nodded. "It's a slow day. You can work extra hours when you feel better."

John pushed himself to his feet, then took a step forward and stopped suddenly.

"You all right?" Charlie asked.

Suddenly John collapsed. Charlie rushed around the desk in a futile effort to catch him before he fell, but to his surprise, John stood up again on his own, holding a pair of bat winged sunglasses that winked with rhinestones. "I nearly stepped on them," John said.

"Good thing you didn't," Charlie replied.

John wiped a hand across his sweating brow. "She'll worry about them. I need to take them to her."

Charlie held out his hand. "No you don't. You go home. If it's that important, then I'll return them. Just tell me where she lives."

John handed the sunglasses over, then fished his car keys out of his pocket while telling Charlie how to find Tilly Reid's house. Charlie turned toward the door. "So I'm not using company time for personal business, I'll just drop these off on my way to take a statement from the petrol station robbery witness."

"Mind you, Tilly and Cat's house is down a little track off the main road," John warned. "Don't give up looking too soon."

"I can go half a mile out of my way, no worries. Take care of yourself."

Chapter 3

Catriona pulled a silent Quigley along the path toward home, his anxious eyes roving from side to side, as if expecting an attack from behind the screen of fresh green leaves growing on the bushes along the path. Something was terribly wrong, and she hated not figuring out just what it was. Birds bustling in the branches overhead seemed to mock her heavy heart. Quigley's wretched feelings of fear and loneliness made no sense to her. What good was it being a visionary if you couldn't see everything you wanted to? "I'm right here," she said in an effort to comfort him. "I won't leave you." Quigley's whimper sent a shiver down Catriona's spine. Perhaps Gran could calm him.

As soon as they drew shouting distance to the house, Quigley circled to stand in front of Catriona. "What has gotten into you?" Catriona asked. "Move it." She gave him a shove, but he steadfastly blocked her way. "You made me drag you all this way, and now you won't let me go in?" She gave him another shove, but Quigley wouldn't get out of her way. When Catriona stepped around him, he circled and pushed in front of her again. "Are you barmy?" Cat's extraordinary sense let her know that the situation was anything but funny. What made him behave so strangely? Was he sick?

"Gran!" she called. "Gran, help! Quigley's going crazy." She looked down at her dog, wondering with a heavy heart if he would ever be her warm and steady friend again.

Catriona glanced at the closed door in frustration. Maybe Gran was in the loo and couldn't come out to help her. Cat forged ahead, pushing past her stubborn dog. On the doorstep, Quigley let out a heart-breaking howl. That decided it. He had to get to the vet. Perhaps he needed pills. Depressed people took pills, so maybe depressed dogs did, too.

The warm spring sun glowed like a gentle caress while Catriona told herself that everything would work out alright, even though deep inside she knew that something was so wrong and that things would never be the same again. Suddenly cold, she trembled as she leaned across Quigley's back and pushed the door open. "Gran!"

Quigley's tail lowered and his ridiculous ears drooped as he stood guard in front of Catriona, who stared in at Gran with her book splayed on her chest, wide eyes staring as if surprised to see them home so soon.

"Gran!" Catriona cried, tripping over Quigley and landing on her hands and knees on the floor. She scrambled up and dashed to Gran, throwing her arms around Gran's warm body. "Gran! Wake up! It's me, Cat!" Tears filled her eyes as Gran remained still, not even a sigh of breath escaping her mouth. "Gran!" Cat cried, burying her face against Gran's shirt. "You're not old enough to die! I don't have anyone but you! Come back! I need you!"

Gran said nothing. There was no sudden start of waking, no reassuring hand on Cat's head.

Something touched Catriona's hand, and she whirled to see Quigley slinking in beside her, his belly nearly touching the ground. "You knew," she sobbed, dropping to the floor and putting her forehead against the dog. "Why didn't I know she was going to die?" Tears ran down her face as she hugged Quigley. "I would have stayed home and called for an ambulance. That's what you wanted me to do, isn't it? You tried to get me to stay and take care of Gran." The ache in her throat pinched off her words. She mouthed, "But I didn't listen," then cried as if she would never stop.

Quigley stiffened and turned his head toward the door, his thin tail wagging in a circle. Cat looked up through wet eyes, fear nearly consuming her as a shadow fell across the floor. Why hadn't she closed the door? A squeal of fear escaped her throat as a pair of broad shoulders filled the doorway, the sunlight shadowing the intruder's features.

"What's happened?" asked Sergeant Walters. Before Catriona could answer, the sergeant strode into the room, knelt at Gran's side, and touched the side of her neck with his fingers.

Cat felt as if every bone in her body turned to straws. She couldn't have stood on her feet if the house was on fire. "Gran won't wake up," she murmured, still holding onto Quigley, who quivered in her arms.

"I'll make a phone call," Walters said softly. Cat listened as he called for an ambulance. Then he squatted down beside her. Quigley wriggled closer to the sergeant with delight as Sergeant Walters asked, "Do you have family close by?"

"No." Suddenly, Cat felt strangely detached from the room and everyone in it.

"Do you have any other family at all?"

"Not that I know of."

"So…she was your grandmother?"

Cat nodded.

"Where's your mother?"

Cat shrugged.

"Do you really not know where your mother is?"

"She left when I was four. I don't remember her."

"I see." The sergeant was quiet a moment before he stood and moved to Gran's book shelf, where Gran had a habit of tucking papers in beside books with just a little bit sticking out. "Did your grandmother have an address book?"

"Sometimes she emailed people on the computer down at the library."

"Do you know her password?"

Cat shook her head. Then she noticed Quigley staring at her with his intelligent brown eyes. "I know," she whispered miserably.

Walters looked back at her. "Know what?"

Catriona's chin quivered. "If I'd stayed here when Quigley wanted me to, I could have called for help. Instead, I went to the police station to show off my stupid glasses."

The sergeant glanced at her glasses on the telephone table where he'd placed them. He returned to Cat and knelt beside her. " You mustn't blame yourself. This isn't your fault. There are lots of reasons people pass away. They can't always be saved, by you, me, or even by the doctors, even if we are right there with them. Do you understand?"

"This is different," Cat said. "Quigley didn't want me to leave, but I did anyway."

"You didn't know this would happen," Walters insisted.

When Catriona dared to look at Quigley again, she saw no censure in his eyes, only love. Maybe the sergeant as right. Maybe Gran would have died even if Cat had been here.

Suddenly, Gran's night time phone call came to mind.. "Marlow," Cat blurted.

"Marlow?"

"Last night Gran was on the phone yelling at someone named Marlow."

"Do you have a last name?"

Cat shook her head.

"Which phone did she use?" Sergeant Walters asked.

"Her mobile."

"Where is it?"

Catriona glanced at Gran's still body. "She keeps it in her pocket."

The sound of approaching vehicles sounded through the doorway. Tires rolled to a stop, engines shut off, doors opened and closed and footfalls hurried toward the house. The emergency medical personnel had arrived.

"Look," Walters said, "I'm going to help take care of things here. Is there someone you know, a friend you can stay with for awhile until we get this all sorted?"

Cat began to shake her head, but then thought of Liam's Uncle Richard and Aunt Sarah, owners of Kane Farms, and she burst into tears. They would take her in.

Chapter 4

"We could postpone our trip," Sarah Kane said to Sergeant Walters with an uncertain twitch of her apron, which sent a small puff of flour into the air, "or we could take Catriona with us." She reached out and circled Cat's shoulders, pulling her close.

"No need," Walters said. "She has an Aunt Marlow in New Jersey who's flying in tomorrow to take over her care."

"Fancy that," Sarah said. "I didn't know there was anyone besides Tilly. What a shock." Sarah dabbed her eyes and bent to look into Cat's face. "Are you alright, dear?"

Cat nodded, feeling safe tucked into Sarah's side. She was still trying to get used to the idea that she had an aunt. Since Marlow was Gran's other daughter, Cat couldn't help picturing her looking like Gran, but wearing American clothes. She hoped Aunt Marlow would be nice, but Gran had been shouting at her, so Cat wasn't entirely sure what to expect.

"Poor Tilly," Sarah continued, "She died all alone."

"It appears to have been very peaceful," Walters said.

"Well, that's a mercy."

"And she'd reached the end of her book," Catriona added.

"Cat, come play with us!" called Sarah's eight-year-old son, Nick. "The dogs are ganging up!"

The sergeant turned toward the Kane's dog, Fido, and Quigley jumping up on Nick. "Uh, oh, sounds like an emergency."

Cat gave Sarah a brief hug before heading towards the melee.

"I'll be back tomorrow to pick you up," Sergeant Walters called after her.

Cat wished she could simply stay here with people who cared about her. But deep inside, in the place where she knew things she didn't want to know, she saw a long, dark road stretching ahead of her, and she couldn't see the end of it.

Chapter 5

Aunt Marlow's anxious eyes, ringed with eyeliner, relaxed when she spied Cat standing outside the Kane's house. Her short hair, the color of brown sugar, barely moved as she walked toward her niece with Sergeant Walters right behind her. Marlow didn't resemble Gran much. Taller and more slender, she looked pretty in spite of deep lines running from her nose to the corners of her mouth.

Stopping in front of Catriona, Marlow's lipstick-coated mouth twitched in what might have been an attempt at a smile. "Well, now, Catriona, is it?"

"Yes." She would not offer to let this woman to call her"Cat." Not yet.

Instead of giving Charlie Walters his usual enthusiastic greeting, Quigley leaned against Cat's side, staring up at Marlow with anxious brown eyes.

"Call me Aunt Marlow. Alright?"

Cat nodded, wishing that she didn't have an Aunt Marlow. Without any relatives, she could live with the Kane's.

Sarah hurried out of the house toward the group, her hand out. "Well, hello there, I'm Sarah Kane."

Marlow took her hand. "Marlow Reid Davies. Thank you for taking my niece in."

"No trouble at all. We'd keep her permanently if we could."

"No need." Marlow let go of Sarah's hand and smiled down at Cat. "She has a home in New Jersey."

Cat felt a cold wash of dread course through her. How could she move to an entirely different country, away from everyone and everything she knew? She grasped Quigley's collar in sudden panic. "Do I have to go?"

"Cat," Sarah gasped. "This is your very own aunt. You don't want to go saying things to hurt her feelings."

22

Marlow stood staring at Cat as if she'd just barked like a dog. Cat dropped her gaze, feeling sick to her stomach. Quigley shifted his weight and sat on her feet.

"It's been a trying time for everyone," Sarah said. "Why don't you all come in for some tea and biscuits?" She led the way toward the house, and Marlow followed.

Sergeant Walters bent down and rubbed Quigley's ears. "Listen," he whispered to Cat. "Change can be hard. Sometimes it's for the best, but you don't know it right off."

"But I do know."

"Oh. Yeah." He raised his eyebrows and smiled. "Well, since she's your only living family we can find, you have to go with her for now."

"Do you have other relatives, Sargeant? Like a wife?"

Walters looked puzzled at her question, but answered, "I've got a mum and dad, a sister and two brothers, and I've got my girl, Ellie. We're to be married in six weeks."

"Then you don't know what it's like to be alone."

"But you aren't alone. Besides your aunt, you've got an uncle and two cousins waiting for you in New Jersey."

Tears welled in Cat's eyes. "Where's Officer Lamb?"

Charlie Walters hesitated, then said, "He wanted to be here, but couldn't make it."

A heavy blanket of sorrow descended over Catriona. "I don't want to leave without seeing him."

"Uh…he's actually in hospital."

Cat's eyes filled with tears.

"He's having good care."

More lonely than ever, Catriona gripped Quigley's collar. She'd felt Officer Lamb's sickness, but hadn't wanted to believe it. Now Gran was dead and Officer Lamb was very sick. It seemed that the only loving thing she had that she could keep was Quigley.

If only Gran had told her about Aunt Marlow, Cat could have gotten used to the idea of having another relative. It would have been nice to see a picture of her, talk with Gran about what Marlow was like as a child, maybe even spend a few minutes on the phone speaking with her aunt. Even hearing her voice once would have helped her feel a connection. Why hadn't Gran prepared her?

"I'll see if I can at least get you John's email address." The sergeant straightened. "You'd better go in."

On impulse, Cat grabbed his hand. "Stay with me."

The sergeant looked surprised, then relaxed. "For a bit."

When they went inside, Catriona took a seat at the end of the table in the cinnamon scented kitchen. Quigley sat steadfastly on the floor beside her. Grateful that he wasn't sitting by Sergeant Walters this afternoon, Cat ate a chocolate biscuit without tasting it while Marlow engaged in conversation about the Kane's berry farm, raising children, and Sarah's husband, Richard, who was away getting supplies for their Australian vacation. While Marlow sounded perfectly friendly, Catriona could not understand the disapproving glances that she gave Quigley. He wasn't even begging.

A sudden beep startled her, and Sergeant Walters jumped up. "I've got to go," he said, fumbling with an electronic device. "Thanks for the tea."

Catriona stood, intending to go out with him, but the sergeant motioned for her to stay. Then he hurried out the door. Catriona's voice sounded small when she asked, "Now what?"

Marlow stood. "We need to stop by Mum's and sort through things. Come with me."

Catriona turned toward Sarah, who gave her an encouraging smile. "There, now, you're all sorted." Sarah stood, walked to Cat and folded her into a warm hug. Cat held on as long as she dared. When she finally let go, Sarah picked up the empty biscuit plate and teapot and headed for the sinkt.

With Quigley at her heels, Catriona turned and followed Marlow to the door.

"Leave him here," Marlow said.

"But he always goes with me," Cat said. "Even to the police station."

"We can sort things better without him underfoot."

Catriona took hold of Quigley's collar and stood still, afraid to let go.

"He's very well behaved," Sarah said. "Don't you think he might go along as a therapy dog for her? She's been through so much."

Marlow's smile tightened. "All right. Come along."

Relieved, Cat followed Marlow out to her rental car and pulled Quigley in on the backseat beside her.

When Marlow turned off the engine and looked out the car window at Gran's house, Cat's stomach froze up at the distaste on her aunt's face. Then Marlow got out of the car and walked inside Gran's house without looking back.

Cat wondered if she even had to go in. The image of Gran's body lying in her chair was still fresh in her mind. But Gran wasn't there anymore, and Marlow had left the house door wide open, so Cat climbed out and walked to the doorway of the only home she'd ever known. Quigley stopped on the doorstep behind her.

"It's worse than I remember," Marlow muttered.

Cat felt heat rising in her cheeks. How dare her aunt talk badly of Gran's home? It's true that it didn't smell like cinnamon and tea, but it was familiar and comforting. Cat couldn't stop herself from asking, "What is worse?"

Marlow turned, looking as surprised as if she'd been pulled back through time. Her gaze flicked from Cat to Quigley. "There's nothing he can ruin in here, so he might as well come in."

Cat didn't move, except to pull herself up as tall as she could, which wasn't much. "What's worse? Do you think something's wrong with Gran's house?"

Marlow flicked her hand. "It's old and dingy. When Dad was alive, he kept it up. I would have at least sent Mum money for paint if I'd known."

"Or you could have come to see her."

Marlow frowned. "Who are you to tell me what to do? Mum understood that I have a life in the United States. Do you know how far away that is? I couldn't come visit her every Sunday. I called her all the time."

"To argue."

Marlow's eyes narrowed. "Is that what she told you?"

"That's what I overheard."

Marlow bit her lips and turned toward the wall. After a moment, she patted her hair and turned back. "Look Catriona, I'm sorry. I didn't mean to say anything to upset you. This is a sad situation for both of us. I've lost my mum, and you lost your Grandmother. I really want you to come and live with us." She made another attempt a smile. "You're almost the same age as your cousin, Tamsin. We live close to New York City, and you can go there if you'd like. It will be quite an adventure. I want to make this work for both of us. Can we please just start over?"

Marlow's words made sense. She had just lost her mother, after all. If she felt even half as miserable as Cat felt without her gran, then Cat could even feel sorry for her.

Catriona moved inside the house with Quigley following her closely, his tail lowered. Suddenly Marlow put her hand out toward Cat. Cat hesitated. Was she going to hug her? Sarah Kane's hug made Cat feel secure, like everything would be all right. A hug from Marlow might help Cat feel better about going to the States. Maybe the dark tunnel she saw whenever she was close to Marlow might suddenly have a light at the end.

Marlow stepped closer and gave Cat's shoulder a single pat. "Friends?"

Cat simply nodded as the brief warmth of Marlow's palm left as if it had never been there.

Chapter 6

Cat didn't think anything could be worse than seeing Gran's coffin braced over a hole in the ground until the next morning when Marlow said, "We're leaving for home in three days."

"Does Quigley need shots?"

Marlow looked puzzled. "How would I know?"

"We need to find out if he's got to have shots to fly on the airplane."

Marlow went still for a moment before saying, "He's not going with us."

A sudden wave of despair crashed over Cat, so heavy that she couldn't breathe. Finally she swallowed enough fear to blurt, "He has to come."

"He can't. We are not an animal family. Tamsin is allergic."

"But he's all I have left."

Marlow put on a smile. "You have us now."

Cat pressed her fingers together. "What if I keep him outside?"

Marlow's eyes went hard. "No."

"There are kennels in New Jersey, aren't there? I'll keep him there. I'll get a job to pay for his care and everything."

"That's enough talk about the dog. He's not coming."

That was the moment Cat decided to run away. She'd take Quigley and hide until Marlow was gone. She could fend for herself until the Kane's got back from Australia. Then she'd move in with them, and work hard on their farm to pay for room and board. If that didn't work out for some reason, then they'd just be on their own, her and Quigley. They could manage.

As soon as Marlow left to list the house with an estate agent, Quigley studied Cat's every move as she packed her rucksack. The final item was Gran's favorite scarf. Rolling it into a tight bundle, Cat pressed it to her nose and took in a breath of Gran's scent before folding it on top of everything and zipping up her pack. She was ready to go.

Quigley suddenly dashed to the window, tail wagging. Cat's heart nearly stopped. Was Aunt Marlow back so soon? Cat pulled on her rucksack and carefully peered between the curtains in time to see Sergeant Walters step out of his patrol car. Did he somehow know what she was up to? Had he come to stop her?

Closing her eyes and taking a deep breath, she knew in a moment that he wasn't after her. He had brought something good.

As soon as she opened the door, Quigley made a mad dash for the sergeant. In an instant, Cat saw that Charlie Walters wasn't alone. A young woman with dark, almond-shaped eyes stepped out of the back of the car and looped her arm through Charlie's, the sun glinting on her long black hair. Next, Charlie opened the passenger door and a pale John Lamb hefted himself out of the seat.

In a rush of love and gratitude, Cat dashed outside behind Quigley, who made a tail-wagging stop before the sergeant as Charlie bent down to greet the squirming dog.

The woman rose a notch in Cat's eyes when she smiled with delight and rubbed Quigley's head with the words, "What a good boy!" Not only was she pretty, but she was kind.

"This is my friend Quigley," Charlie said to her.

The woman cupped Quigley's face in her slender hands. "He's so cute."

Clearly smitten, Quigley wiggled his whole backside in appreciation.

"Hello, Cat," Charlie called. "This is my friend Ellie Chu."

Ellie straightened and gave Cat a friendly wave. "It's so nice to meet you."

Cat waved back as she hurried toward Officer Lamb. As soon as she wrapped her arms around him, she felt a cold rush go through her. Drawing back, she studied his ashen face. "You should be in hospital."

"I couldn't let you leave without seeing you."

"Come in and sit down. Please." Cat tugged him into the house. As soon as he was settled on the couch, she said, "I'll get you some bicarbonate."

Charlie and Ellie followed through the open doorway. "Can I help?" Ellie asked.

"No. Thank you. You can sit." They sat, and Quigley snuggled in beside Charlie's legs.

Cat brought Officer Lamb the bicarbonate and sat beside him, watching anxiously as he drank it, twisting up his features at the sharp tang of it on his tongue. "Thank you," he said, handing the glass back to Cat. "Now, I have something for you." He reached into his pocket and pulled out a piece of paper. Taking Cat's hand, he tucked the paper into it. "Here's my email address. I'd better hear from you so I don't have to come clear across the ocean to check that you are behaving yourself."

Tears rose in Cat's eyes. "I don't want to go."

John put his arm around her. "You'll have Quigley with you. You can email me any time, and when you know your phone number, give it to me, and I'll call you."

"She won't let me take Quigley."

"What?" John sounded outraged. "Who won't let you?"

"Aunt Marlow."

"Why ever not?"

"She says her daughter's allergic."

Quigley left Charlie, trotted over to Cat, and put his head on her lap.

"I'm sorry," John said, giving Cat a squeeze. "I don't see how it can be helped."

"I can't just leave him," Cat said, bending over Quigley's head so that her brown curls touched his blond fur.

"I'll look after him for you," Charlie offered.

Cat looked up to see Ellie's dark eyes, soft with compassion, watching her.

"We could keep him for you until we figure out a way for you to be together," Charlie finished.

"Do you think that could really happen?" Cat asked with rising hope. "That I could be with Quigley again?"

"There's got to be something we can do," Ellie assured her. "We just need time to figure it out."

Cat thought about her plan to run away. She imagined sleeping under bushes and eating berries to survive. She'd forgotten to pack a trowel to dig up roots, and wasn't entirely sure which roots could be eaten. And what about the bathroom? She could use public washrooms for the most part, but where would she clean her clothes if she didn't have money for a laundrette? Even if she washed clothes in a stream, how would she get them dry without anyone noticing? It all suddenly seemed so overwhelming that she threw her arms around Quigley. With tears spilling from her eyes, she whispered, "Do you want to stay with Charlie?"

Quigley let out a gentle whine and pressed his head in toward Cat. She looked up with a shaky smile. "He wants to stay with you."

Ellie's long black hair swayed as she stood. Crossing the room, she knelt beside Cat. "It's going to be all right," she said, putting a hand on Cat's knee.

Cat looked into Ellie's exotic eyes, wanting to believe her, but the darkness and pain rolling over her from the bleak tunnel of her future blocked all optimism.

She was suddenly aware of John Lamb's arm over her shoulders, meant to be comforting, but feeling more like a metal bar. Thinking of getting on a plane with Aunt

Marlow only darkened the sense of her future. Even though Marlow insisted that she wanted Catriona to live with them, something twisted beneath her words, something that wasn't true.

How much did the deception matter? Was it a small omission, or a big lie that would made Cat's life miserable? Cat clenched her hands. Why did she have to be a visionary? She didn't want to sense what was going to happen, to be responsible to deal with ominous feelings and not know who to tell, not even know how to put them into words.

"Aw, honey," Ellie said as she studied Cat's troubled expression. "Quigley is still all yours. He'll just be on vacation with us for awhile."

Catriona stood with a weary slump of her shoulders. "Officer Lamb, you need to go back to hospital."

Chapter 7

Cat followed her aunt onto the airplane and sat where she was told, glad it wasn't a window seat. She wouldn't be able to stop herself from looking out at her homeland dropping steadily below her, falling further and further behind, leaving only a cold empty ocean beneath her. Cat sat hunched in her seat, clutching her rucksack with her old multicolored hat inside. Charlie had brought it when he collected Quigley. "John felt terrible you couldn't take your dog," Charlie explained. "He knows it's not the same, but he thought you might want to have this with you."

As the plane took off, Cat slid her hand inside her pack and fingered the little bells sewn onto the fringe of yarn that once circled her head, their gentle jingling softening the impact of her visions. They didn't drown out her misery now. Even when she managed to fall asleep with her head tipped back against the airplane seat, she dreamed of Quigley sitting alone on the side of the road. Although she was desperate to reach him, no matter how hard she tried, she couldn't get to him.

After the plane landed, they made their way through the John F. Kennedy airport labyrinth to the baggage claim area. Marlow approached a tall, thin man with anxious eyes, his receding brown hair combed back from his high forehead. "Hello, Archie," Marlow greeted him. "Here she is." Turning to Catriona, Marlow said, "This is your Uncle Archie."

As Archie nodded, Cat felt a wave of sad hopelessness roll off him and touch her with its gray coldness. With a little shiver, Cat studied his face, wondering what could be making him feel that way. Was it something that she would have to feel every time she was around him? She fingered the zipper on her rucksack, wondering if she could pull out her hat and put it on to help block out his feelings.

"Did Mum teach you nothing?" Marlow said. "Can't you say hello?"

Cat gave a start at Marlow's disapproving tone. "Hello," she said, looking into Archie's fathomless eyes.

When Marlow turned and strode toward the luggage carousels, Archie followed. Cat took advantage of having no eyes trained on her to pull the hat from her pack and stuff it into her jacket pocket before trailing after Archie, who appeared to be trying to read his wife's mind. Cat did not miss the fact that Archie hadn't tried to put an arm around his wife or make an attempt at a welcoming kiss. Even though Cat's experience with husbands and wives was limited to Richard and Sarah Kane, she had not expected such coolness from a married couple who'd been apart for several days. Imagining Richard and Sarah meeting, even after one day, she was sure they would give one another hugs along with some good-natured teasing.

This cold reception made her so uneasy that she wanted to hug Quigley, but since he wasn't there, she gripped her colorful cap instead.

Marlow pointed out her two rolling suitcases and Archie retrieved them before glancing at Catriona. "Do you have any other bags?"

Cat shook her head and gripped the straps of her rucksack where they rested over each shoulder. Archie offered her a small smile. "It's nice that you can pack light."

"How's Tamsin?" Marlow asked as she led the way on a rapid march toward the exit.

"The same," Archie replied, straining to keep up while carrying some of his wife's bags while pulling others behind him.

"Where did you park?

"Short term parking, first level," Archie said. Glancing back to make sure Catriona was still following, he gave her an encouraging smile, which lifted Cat's spirits a bit.

When they reached the car, Marlow headed for the driver's seat. Archie sat in the passenger side, and Cat got in by herself in the back, staring out at the tall buildings crowding the skyline as she clutched her colorful hat. They headed south, eventually crossing a huge bridge. The tall buildings diminished as they left the city and drove along a route that took them to Hamilton, New Jersey.

By the time they pulled into the driveway of a two story house that was easily three times bigger than Gran's, Cat was so tired that all she wanted to do was curl up and sleep. Trailing her aunt and uncle into the house, she almost followed Archie, dragging Marlow's luggage, through a set of double doors. When Marlow put her arm around Cat's shoulders to stop her, Cat figured they must lead to the master bedroom. Relaxing into her aunt's welcome touch, Cat murmured, "I'm tired."

"Of course you are, dear. Your room is right here." Marlow led Cat to a tall door painted butter yellow and knocked. How odd. Why would she knock on a guest room door? Then a voice inside said softly, "Who is it?"

"Your mother," Marlow replied in a gentle voice, pushing the door open and leading Cat into a room that smelled of menthol and vanilla.

On a canopied bed, covered with a frosted white spread, lay the most beautiful girl Cat had ever seen. Her glossy caramel-streaked hair spread out over a blush colored pillow just like Sleeping Beauty's would have if she were real. The girl struggled to sit up, her unnaturally pale skin adding to her unearthly beauty. Blue eyes lighting up, she asked, "Is that her?"

"Yes, this is your cousin, Catriona."

"Come here," the girl said, patting the side of her bed with a hand that looked too large for its thin arm.

When Cat hesitated, Marlow shifted a white metal walker from the side of the bed and gave Cat a gentle nudge. "Go on, go see Tamsin. She's looked forward to meeting you for such a long time."

Cat slowly lowered herself onto the edge of the bed. It was hard to believe she was related to this vision of beauty. Yet she sensed something tenuous about Tamsin, something insubstantial. Before she could figure out what it was, Tamsin asked, "So how do your powers work?"

With a creeping sense of dread, Cat asked, "What?"

"How does it work? You know, seeing things, knowing what's going to happen, changing the future."

Cat glanced back at Marlow, whose smile tightened. "I...I don't know."

Tamsin took Cat's hand with a grip as light as butterfly wings. "It doesn't matter. We'll be great friends. I'm glad you're my cousin. It's so exciting to finally meet you. You don't snore, do you?"

Cat didn't understand why she was asking until she caught sight of a narrow twin bed pushed against the far wall. The blue and white striped spread was nice enough, but it didn't match the room. "I'm sleeping in here?"

"Of course," Marlow said.

Cat had never shared a room before, so didn't know how it was supposed to be done. Right now it didn't seem to matter if there were rules, because at the sight of her assigned bed, she felt a nearly overpowering urge to collapse onto it, close her eyes, and pull the covers over her head as a shield against this unfamiliar place.

Marlow cut across a corner of the room to open a door in the bedroom wall. "This is Tamsin's bathroom. You may use it if you keep it clean. If you have bad habits, you need to use the one at the back of the house next to the mud room."

Tamsin's door suddenly burst open, and a tall young man with wavy, cream-colored hair burst in. The wide white smile beneath his classically straight nose was genuine, making Cat instantly want to smile back. If not for this garish green circus shirt, he would look like a male model. "Is she here yet?" he asked at the same moment he caught sight of Catriona. When he turned his head, she noticed a bright red stain on the left side of his neck that crept up over the edge of his perfectly chiseled square jaw.

"Get out, Barrett!" Tamsin squealed.

At the same time, Marlow said sharply, "You know you're supposed to knock!"

Barrett cheerfully rapped his knuckles on the inside of the door, then approached Catriona. "Hi. I'm your cousin, Barrett. Do you hug?" He put his arms out, and Cat stepped into them without hesitation. When he wrapped her in a gentle hug, Cat felt warm and welcome for the first time since she'd left Quigley behind.

"Oh, for goodness' sake, Barrett, let go," Marlow scolded. "You haven't known her long enough. I wish you would act your age."

"I'm seventeen," Barrett said, pulling back from Cat and looking down at her.

"I'm thirteen," Cat replied with a grateful smile. "You can call me 'Cat.'"

A wide grin spread across Barrett's handsome face. "Absolutely. I like that name. Cat. It's soft and warm."

In a calmer voice, Marlow said, "Look, Barrett, why don't you go and color? I got some new pictures for you."

"Thank you, Mother, but I don't do crayons anymore. I'm a painter now." Barrett turned toward Tamsin. "Before I go, how are you feeling, Tam?"

"It's Tamsin," his sister snapped.

Barrett rubbed his ear. "You liked 'Tam' when we were kids, and I liked you calling me 'Bear.'"

"Well, unlike you, I'm not a kid anymore."

Cat didn't understand Tamsin's harshness toward Barrett, but through it all, his smile never faded.

"As you wish," Barrett said cheerfully. "How do you feel today, Tamsin?"

"Same as always."

"Would you like a hug?" Barrett put his arms out toward her.

"No! Don't come any closer."

Barrett's smile faltered, but he found it again as he dropped his arms to his sides. "I love you, Tam."

"Don't call me that!"

"Sorry, I forgot. How about you, Mother?" Barrett held his arms out toward Marlow.

She hesitated, then took hold of one of his hands and patted it. "Look, go change your shirt. You've got better ones to wear." Her nose wrinkled slightly with distaste. "Then you can use the twisty crayons to color."

"I'd rather paint."

Barrett turned to Cat. "Do you want to paint with me?"

"No, Barrett," Marlow said. "Catriona is too tired to paint." She smiled and put an arm around Cat.

"Absolutely," Barrett said. "Sleeping's good for the soul."

Barrett's words were so agreeable, and Marlow's touch felt so nice that Cat wondered if she'd found a complete family at last. Didn't most families have disagreements now and then? She missed Gran, of course, and Quigley was missing from the picture, too. She couldn't do anything about Gran, but maybe if she made a place for herself here, Cat could find a way to get Quigley back. She yawned. "May I go to bed?"

Tamsin's face scrunched up in disappointment. "But it's only five o'clock."

"Where she's from, it's more like ten o'clock at night," Marlow explained.

"So what am I supposed to do?" Tamsin pouted, which made her look winsome rather than spoiled. "I'm not even tired yet."

"Well," Marlow sounded uncertain. "You could read a book."

"Or we could play Mouse Trap!" Barry offered with great enthusiasm.

Tamsin flicked him a disapproving glance. "Mother."

"Barrett, you know Tamsin doesn't care for that game."

Unable to suppress her curiosity, Cat asked, "Why do you play with mousetraps?"

Barrett's eyes lit up. "Oh, a Cat playing Mousetrap!" he said. "You could play, and with a name like yours, you're bound to win."

"She's supposed to stay in my room and help me," Tamsin said.

"She will, darling," Marlow assured her.

"Hi, girls," Archie said as he pushed the door open wider. "Oh, hello, Barrett. I didn't see you there."

Barrett's movie star smile beamed. "Hi, Dad."

Archie moved to his daughter's bedside and lightly stroked her arm. "How are you feeling tonight?"

"I'm not tired, Daddy, but Catriona wants to sleep, so what am I supposed to do? Sit here and watch her lying in bed like a lump?"

"Well, Cat could sleep, and I could play a game with you until you're tired."

"Mouse Trap!" Barrett offered.

Tamsin rolled her eyes. "No."

"Then Dad can play with me!"

"First things first, son. I think it would be best if we have Catriona sleep in my office for tonight."

"But we arranged this," Marlow said, indicating the twin bed.

"She should have a quiet place to sleep until she's adjusted to the time zone," Archie said. "Come along, Catriona." He held a hand toward her. "I'll show you where to sleep."

"There aren't any clean blankets up here." Marlow's hands settled on her hips. "They're all in the wash."

"We'll make do." Archie took a step toward the twin bed. "We'll just borrow these."

Marlow blocked his way. "No need to mess those up. She'll be in here tomorrow. She can use a sleeping bag for one night, can't she?"

"She could," Archie agreed, "but don't you think she'd be more comfortable with real sheets?"

Curiously light-headed, Cat looked from her aunt to her uncle and murmured, "I don't mind."

"Let me help." Barrett took Cat's hand. "Dad, you can fold out the couch and we'll get the bedding."

Barrett led Cat out of the room to the kitchen where he opened a door that revealed wodden steps leading down to a concrete floor. A furnace and water heater faced off in opposite corners, while a washer and dryer waited beneath narrow shelves crowded with soap, fabric softener, and dryer sheets. Two small windows looked out over fresh spring grass pressing against the edge of thel panes.

Rounding the bottom of the stairs to follow Barrett, the vague scent of laundry soap and pine cleaner reached Cat's nose. Lidded storage boxes stacked beneath the stairs bore labels such as "Christmas decorations," "Tamsin winter clothes," and "costumes." Piled around the boxes were picnic coolers, skis, and a tricycle. The whole basement felt so cramped and lonely that Cat wrapped her arms around herself, feeling colder than a New Year's night in Salisbury.

Barrett bent, opened the dryer, and pulled out a fluffy comforter. "Here," he said, wrapping it around Cat's shoulders. "You look cold."

"Thanks."

"You go ahead up to the kitchen," Barrett said, pointing to the stairs. "I'll follow with the sheets and turn out the light so you don't have to be down here in the dark."

Cat stumbled up the stairs with Barrett close behind her. "Dad's office is nice," Barrett said, closing the basement door. "I can go in there to read if he's not there and I don't mess things up."

Guiding Cat through a door at the end of the hallway, they found Archie unfolding the hide-a-bed of a brown leather couch with a practiced pull. Cat barely noticed the heavy drapes across a wide single window, the desk, or wall of shelves filled with books. While Barrett helped put sheets on the mattress, he said, "I told Cat you don't mind her being here if she doesn't mess things up. Right, Dad?"

"That's right."

"So be sure you keep things neat, Cat. Mom says cleanliness is next to Godliness. But God's never been here as far as I know."

"Remember, this is just for tonight," Marlow said, appearing in the doorway while shaking a pillow down into a pillow case. "Tomorrow you'll be where you belong."

Cat felt a tug of loneliness overshadow her fatigue. She wished she could be back where she really belonged, back home in Salisbury.

"The extra bathroom is down the hall to the right."

"I'll show you," Barrett offered.

So while Marlow tossed the pillow on the bed and Archie shook out the comforter, Barrett led Cat to the small bathroom beside the back door at the rear of the house. Besides an aqua colored toilet and sink, there was a cozy shower tucked in the corner behind a frosted glass door. It was perfectly lovely. Cat managed to use the facilities, change into her pink and yellow pajama shorts and top, and brush her teeth without falling asleep. Then she stumbled out of the bathroom where Barrett waited to lead her back to the office. Cat sank gratefully onto the bed, closed her eyes, and was asleep in a moment. Barrett made sure she was covered before quietly leaving the room and closing the door behind him.

Chapter 8

Quigley galloped toward Cat, skidding to a stop at her feet and wagging his tail furiously. Falling to her knees, Cat hugged her dog, feeling the warmth of his skin, hearing his breath in her ear. "I missed you so much."

Quigley nuzzled her hair, then pulled back and crouched down with his front quarters on the ground, his hind end up in the air with his tail rolling crazily. "Oh, you want to play, do you?" Cat asked in delight. She made a grab for him. He dodged out of the way. She laughed and lunged for him again, thrilled with their game of tag. "You're a good boy, aren't you?"

"He's good when you're around."

Cat looked up to see Charlie standing over them. Where had he come from? "What's he like when I'm not here?"

Charlie folded his arms and shot a look at Quigley. "Kind of mopey. Spends a lot of time staring toward the west."

Cat caught hold of her prancing dog and rubbed the fur behind his ears. "I want to be with him all the time."

"I don't blame you for that. How are things with your family in the States?"

"Strange. They argue, and I think there's something wrong with my cousins. Tamsin's one of those who doesn't eat enough, or else she's sick with something that's wasting her away. Even though Barrett is seventeen, his mother told him he should color pictures, like he was more child than man. But neither of them look like there's much wrong with them, except for Barrett's red birthmark."

"Hm. Does the arguing escalate into violence? Has anyone hurt you?"

"No."

Charlie tapped his chin. "It usually takes time to get to know people and get used to a new place."

"I just want to come home."

41

Charlie squatted down beside Cat. "Have you ever wondered if there's something you're supposed to do for your family?"

Cat was silent.

"You know you're a special girl, right?"

"I don't feel special."

"But you are. You're able to do things not many people can. Maybe this move to the States is more about helping them than you."

Cat looked up into Sergeant Charlie Walters' dark eyes. "What am I supposed to do?"

Charlie shrugged. "If you keep your head up and look for it, you might find what it is faster than if you're always looking down and wishing to be someplace else."

Quigley rolled onto his side so Cat could scratch his tummy. "Why is it so hard?"

"It's all in how you look at it," Charlie said, hunkering down beside her. "Some people think it's too difficult to climb a mountain, while others can't wait to hit the slope. Is it hard to learn piano? Some think so, others love to practice. It was hard for you to come to the police station at first, but you helped us, and made friends. Look here," he held out his arms. "Because you did something that was hard to do, you've got me on your side."

"And Officer Lamb."

Charlie's face sobered. "And John, yes. He'd hate to think you weren't happy. For his sake, can you try to see all of this as a grand adventure?"

Cat sighed. "Only if I'll be going back home at the end of it."

"It's always possible."

"I'll do my best."

Cat woke up with the phantom feeling of Quigley's fur beneath her fingers. She rolled over on an unfamiliar bed and opened her eyes to ghostly moonlight illuminating a towering bookcase as wide as the wall.

Then she remembered. She was in Uncle Archie's study.

Even though it was clearly night here in Hamilton, her body told her it was morning. Should she should wait until the rest of the household was up before she got out of bed? Then she realized she couldn't wait because her full bladder and empty stomach were both complaining too much.

After using the bathroom, she quietly made her way down the hall toward the kitchen. Surely no one would mind if she ate a slice of bread or two.

She never made it to the bread box, because just before stepping through the kitchen door, she heard Aunt Marlow say, "I'm telling you, Archie, this weird child of Linnea's just might prove useful after all."

"For goodness' sake, Marlow, she's not here to be used. She's an orphan in need of a family."

"But she's no ordinary child, Archie. She's a visionary. Don't you know what that means?"

"I know the definition, but I don't know what it means to someone who is one."

Marlow's voice filled with emotion. "It means that she can see a way to cure Tamsin."

"Is that how it works?" Archie asked. "Do you really know what she can do? Or even what she wants to do? It isn't right to just use people however you want. They have feelings, too."

"But she's family. Families are supposed to help one another. That's why we took her in, to help her, and in return, she'll help Tamsin."

Archie let out a weary sigh. "Why is it that you spend more time trying to help our daughter than our son?"

After a brief silence, Marlow said tersely, "I don't know what you're talking about. I've done all I can for Barrett."

"By taking him out of school? How did that help?"

"Archie, how can you even ask? You know he came home with bruises and a torn shirt. What did you want me to do? Leave him there to be tortured?"

"Boys play rough. He didn't complain. When he was in school, he was getting an education, and he had some friends."

Marlow's voice dropped. "All his so-called friends were in the slow class. How would that have helped him find a job and get along in the world?"

"How is he supposed to get along on his own by living at home?"

"I teach him."

"By giving him crayons and coloring pages?"

"I do the best I can, Archie. If you think you could do any better, then go ahead."

"I didn't want him out of school in the first place. Since I'm gone so much, it seems I didn't get any say in it."

"You're right."

In the silence that followed, Cat turned, ready to make her way back to the office.

"Well, I got up to catch a plane," Archie said to the sound of scraping chair legs. "I've got to get tot he airport."

"That's why I have to take care of everything."

Archie sounded tired when he said, "Marlow, I'm doing the best I can."

Catriona hurried back down the hallway as fast as she could go. Was this the grand adventure Charlie had talked about in her dream? She didn't feel adventurous, she felt unwanted.

One thing Archie was right about is that Marlow didn't know anything about Cat's abilities. Cat couldn't conjure up a vision anytime she wanted. If it were up to her, she'd never have them. She didn't know how to cure Tamsin. She didn't even know what was wrong with her. What would happen when Aunt Marlow found out that Cat couldn't do what she wanted her to do?

Cat slipped back into the office, her hunger overshadowed by confusion and fear. Sinking down onto the fold-out bed, she closed her eyes and wished she had powers that would transport her back to England.

What should she do now? If only she could talk it over with someone. Charlie had talked to her in her dream, but he didn't know her as well as Officer Lamb did. John Lamb would know what to say to help her.

Cat dug her hat with the bells out and bunched it on her lap, thinking. She didn't have a phone, but even if she did, she didn't know his number. Phone calls across the ocean probably cost a lot of money. Should she write him a letter? Then Cat's gaze settled on the computer sitting on Archie's desk. There was her solution. She'd memorized John Lamb's email address, so she'd send him an email.

She jumped up, then suddenly feeling dizzy, dropped back down on the bed. Then she made herself rise more slowly and sat in the luxuriously padded desk chair facing the ominously dark screen. If there was a password, she wouldn't be able to send her message.

Grabbing the mouse, Cat watched the dark screen light up, showing a scene of a snow-covered mountain. It certainly wasn't from New Jersey, at least not what she'd seen of it. When Cat clicked the Internet icon, a window flashed open, and she relaxed back into the chair.

Logging into her email, Cat typed in Officer Lamb's email address and told him what she'd overheard, ending with, "Do I have to stay if they don't really want me? I mean, they want me to fix Tamsin, but they don't really want me." Once she hit "send," she felt better, as if an elephant-sized weight had been lifted off her. A burst of optimism overtook her so strongly that she snuck out of the office again and headed quietly for the kitchen, determined to get something to eat.

Chapter 9

Although his eyes were closed, when Charlie Walters felt something watching him, he shot up in bed, startled to find Quigley staring intently at him from his bedside. As his heart settled down in his chest, Charlie asked, "Do you have to go out, boy?"

Quigley cocked his head, a gesture that reminded Charlie of his dream where a smiling Cat played with Quigley. Charlie sank back on his pillow, recalling Cat's yearning to return to England. He wished he could have brought her home with him, just as he had taken Quigley in, but there were laws he had to abide by.

It was just a dream anyway. Charlie's brow furrowed, and he slid his hands behind his head, staring at the ceiling. It hadn't felt like other dreams he'd had. It seemed as if he'd actually seen Cat outside on the lawn and spoken to her. He hoped that what he'd said helped. Then he shook himself and pushed his legs over the side of the bed. It didn't do any good to give advice to a dream person.

Charlie got up and moved toward the kitchen with Quigley right behind him. "There now, boy, will it be kibble or bacon and eggs you'll be wanting?" After the two of them ate, with Quigley slurping up the bacon grease that Charlie poured over his kibble, Charlie went outside to play frisbee catch. It didn't seem to matter if Charlie feinted one way, then heaved it in the opposite direction, Quigley was always there to grab it in his teeth, as if he knew beforehand which way the disc was going to fly. "Smart dog," Charlie admitted as he led Quigley back into the house. "Now you be a good boy while I go to work. No surfing the web, you hear? I'll be back at noon to check on you." He ruffled Quigley's ears and stepped outside.

On his drive to work, Charlie found himself thinking of Cat again. Gripping the steering wheel, he told himself to stop fixating on that dream. There were real cases he had to work with real people and real problems.

He was disappointed to see that John Lamb was still out. On his last visit to him in hospital, he'd promised to check his colleague's messages. Sitting at John's desk and opening his file, he determined to do whatever it took to lessen John's work load. If anything new came in, he'd shove it off on someone else or take care of it himself.

When he logged into John's account, he was pleased to find a message from Cat. Yet when he opened it, he read it with mounting dread.

"I hope you are feeling better, because when I think of you, I feel a black cloud over my head, and my chest hurts. I don't want anything to be wrong with you. You're the only friend I have, besides Quigley.

"I dreamed about Quigley. That makes me not miss him so much. I dreamed about Charlie, too. He said to make the best of it, but he doesn't understand. Last night my aunt told my uncle that she wants me here to cure my cousin, Tamsin. My aunt doesn't really want me at all, she just wants what she thinks I can do. But I don't know how to cure anyone! If I did, Gran would be alive right now. What should I do? I'm scared. Will they put me I out on the street if I don't cure her? I don't have enough money for a ticket back to England. Tell me what to do, because Charlie doesn't know me. I'm not sure he likes me. I hope he's taking good care of Quigley.

"Thanks for the hat. I wore it to bed last night and it helped me feel a little better. Do I have to stay if they don't want me? Can you bring me home?"

Charlie sat back and stared at the ceiling. Catriona had dreamed of him the same night he dreamed of her, and it seemed as if she'd somehow heard what he'd said in his dream. A chill slid down his back. If she didn't have visionary powers, then what was that all about? And what kind of crazy situation had she landed in?

He focused his gaze on the computer screen again. More importantly, what could he do to help her? He couldn't go to America and bring her back, could he? No crime had been committed, at least none that he knew of.

He sat forward and began typing.

"Cat, I'm glad you wrote. First of all, let me know immediately if you are being mistreated. Has anyone hurt you or threatened to hurt you? Don't worry about Quigley. While he misses you, he's getting along, eating good food and exercising every day. Last night, he must have dreamed about you, too, beca..."

The door burst open and the desk officer stood white-faced in the doorway. "We just heard from the hospital that John has been taken to emergency surgery."

Charlie jumped up, then remembered his message to Cat. He had to know if she was being abused. He clicked "send," then rushed out the door.

Chapter 10

"Barrett, what have you done?" Marlow's voice was so full of despair that Cat looked up from loading the dishwasher. Smudged with dirt, Barrett sported a bruise on his cheek, his hair was out of place, and his button-up shirt was torn from hem to ribcage, showing his circus t-shirt underneath.

"Mom, I was just out with some friends," Barrett said, turning away from his mother.

A shiver of warning slid through Cat. Barrett wasn't telling the whole truth.

"You keep saying boys are messy." Barrett fumbled with his shirt buttons.

"What are the names of these friends?" Marlow demanded. "Who are their parents? Where do they live?"

"I don't know everything. They're just friends, okay?" Barrett turned back to his mother and shot his fist out toward her.

She drew back, screaming, "Barrett!"

Barrett looked startled. "It's called 'knuckles,' Mom. You just tap your knuckles against mine." He gave her a hopeful smile. "Try it."

"That's barbaric."

"My friends do it all the time."

Marlow's voice was hard when she said, "They're not your friends."

Barrett dropped his fist, his shoulders slumping. "I'm going to change."

Barrett hurried past Cat, close enough that she saw a faint line of rope burn on his neck.

Troubled, she turned away and awkwardly pushed more dishes into the dishwasher. Gran hadn't had one, because it wasn't hard to keep up with the dishes when there were just two of them. Some of their happiest times had been working together in the kitchen.

"That's not right," Marlow said, pulling Cat's warm memories away from Gran. "You've got to face all the dishes inward or they won't get clean. Haven't you ever seen a dishwasher before?"

Cat curled in on herself and rearranged the dishes the best she could. Then she started the machine and hurried down the hall, nearly bumping into Barrett, who'd put on fresh clothes and combed his hair. Startled, Cat blurted, "Why did you call them your friends?"

Barrett put out his fist. Cat looked at it, then made a fist and tapped it against Barrett's knuckles. He grinned. "Because they are." When Cat simply stared at him, he sighed. "I want them to be my friends. I don't know why they get so rough sometimes." He rubbed his chin. "Maybe they wish they had a special mark like mine." He moved his hand so that his large strawberry birthmark was in full view. Seeing the whole thing for the first time, Cat gasped. It appeared to be the silhouette of Quigley, including his ears that stuck out.

"It's amazing, isn't it?" Barrett asked. "Mother doesn't like it, and some people make fun of it. But I think it helps make other people feel better." Barrett looked down at his foot scuffing against the carpet. "I want to make Tam feel better, too, but she won't let me hug her anymore. She did when we were kids. Why won't she let me now?" Turning his head toward his sister's closed bedroom door, he said, "I'll miss my sister." A tear rolled down his cheek.

Cat's gaze turned toward Tamsin's door, which appeared to opening slowly of its own accord. Oddly enough, instead of seeing a pale, beautiful girl lying helpless on a princess bed, she watched Tamsin run past the doorway, her feet skimming through a grassy field dotted with gloriously colored flowers. The foliage swayed with every joyous leap Tamsin made, her radiant face glowing with a smile. She ran into a lush green park where people sat on benches, walked smooth, clean paths, or pushed children on swings. One after another, they opened their arms to Tamsin, who eagerly entered their embraces. Then Tamsin picked up a dropped child's toy, helped lay out a picnic blanket, and spun some laughing children on a merry go round.

After a long moment of staring at the door, Barrett turned back toward Cat and put an arm around her shoulder. "Will you be my sister?"

Tamsin's doorway filled in with its regular wooden door, and Cat blinked. Then she looked up at Barrett. "I'll be your cousin, which is just as good as a sister, or even better."

"Better?" Barrett asked doubtfully. "I didn't know there was anything better than brother and sister."

Cat took Barrett's hand and held his gaze. "I'm your family, and I'll stick by you."

Barrett's face softened. "Absolutely!" In one swoop, he picked Cat up and held her in a joyous hug. Cat hugged him back, because his arms were warm and strong, and she felt his love. But she couldn't relax in Barrett's embrace, because it also brought with it the image of prison bars.

Chapter 11

"Now, remember, Catriona, your cousin Tamsin wants you to have a sleepover in her room tonight," Marlow said in a voice that was higher than normal. "Don't you, Tamsin?"

"Only if she doesn't snore."

"I'm really tired," Cat said.

"It's not time to sleep yet," Marlow pulled out a drawer and lifted out a hairbrush. "You need to get used to our time zone. Styling Tamsin's hair will help you stay awake for another hour or two."

"But don't pull it," Tamsin said, eyeing the brush. "Start at the bottom and work your way up. Be gentle with the tangles. I want my hair braided, then undone so I can feel the hair fall back down around my shoulders."

Not seeing the point of creating a hairdo just to take it out again, Cat reluctantly took the brush. Could she even make a braid? She'd never done it to her own hair, and Gran's hair was short, so the subject of braiding had never come up.

Cat moved closer to Tamsin's bedside and began brushing the ends of her hair. Marlow gave the girls a satisfied smile. "How about if I bring you something to drink. Would you like some chocolate milk?"

"Hot chocolate," Tamsin said, "with whipped cream, but not too hot so the cream melts." She made a face. "Then I won't drink it."

"I'll be back."

Marlow left as Cat continued to work her way around Tamsin's hair the best she could. "Are you really brushing the ends all the way around before you go any higher?" Tamsin asked.

Cat shrugged. "I thought that's what you told me to do."

"Don't you know anything? You're supposed to brush a whole section from the bottom to the top, then go to the next section and do it again. Don't you ever brush your hair?"

Cat shook her head, making her curls bounce half-heartedly. She'd never done much with her hair, except to wash it and stuff it under a cap.

"Maybe you could wear a hat," Cat suggested.

Tamsin spread her arms. "In bed?"

"Don't you ever get up?"

"Only to go to the bathroom."

"Why?"

"Duh. Because I'm sick."

"What's wrong with you?"

"What's wrong with you?" Tamsin echoed.

Cat didn't say anything for three long strokes of the brush. Then she said, "I see things."

"Everyone sees things!" Tamsin said. "If you don't stop being annoying, I'm going to tell my mother I don't want you here."

Cat dropped the brush onto the blanket. "Well, I don't want to be here. And the things I see aren't just what you see around you. I see visions, things that are going to happen."

Tamsin's eyes lit up with interest. "Mother told me you saw visions, but I thought she was just giving me a cheering up talk. What do you see happening to me?"

Cat clasped her hands, trying not to think about Tamsin running through that ethereal landscape. "First tell me what's wrong with you."

Tamsin's face twisted up into a petulant scowl. "I don't know how to pronounce it. It's some kind of stupid wasting disease. Each day I feel weaker, which makes it harder to walk or to hold onto things. It's really stupid."

"I'm sorry," Cat said. "I could tell it was something like that when I came into your room."

Tamsin's eyes shone. "Really? Is there, like, an aura around me or something?"

Cat put her hands up into the air, palms down, as if pushing lightly on spider webs. "It's more like a feeling in the air, a sense of weakness, a thread of despair."

"That would be coming from my mother. At least, that's how she was until you came along."

Cat dropped her hands. "But I'm not a healer."

"Then you'd better become one in a hurry. Now tell me…"

Marlow pushed the door open with her back, her hands full, holding a tray with two cups of hot chocolate, topped with whipped cream. "Here you go, girls," she said. "Hot chocolate break."

With her mother in the room, Tamsin didn't ask any more about visions. Cat managed to stay awake for another hour, brushing Tamsin's hair under the watchful eye of Aunt Marlow. When she admitted that she couldn't braid hair, Marlow gave her a lesson, but Cat only got the part about crossing one strand of hair over another, so Marlow had to do the braid. Then it was Cat's job to take it out.

Cat finally dropped the brush and said, "I need to sleep."

Marlow folded her hands in her lap. "Well, then, you may use Tamsin's bathroom. The yellow towels are yours."

Cat walked into a large bathroom covered with white tiles, with just a border of pale yellow marching around the backsplash of the sink and around the shower at hip level. It felt like a big, cold cave. Cat got ready for bed, carefully avoiding the white towels, drying her hands on the corner of a yellow one before stumbling back into the bedroom. She headed directly for her little bed, fell into it, and pulled her covers up, the scent of unfamiliar laundry detergent making her feel as if she didn't belong. The last thing she heard before falling asleep was someone saying, "What normal girl in this world doesn't know how to braid hair?"

She awoke to darkness, feeling cold and alien under the blanket that wasn't enough, with sheets that didn't have the proper smell, lying on a bed that didn't feel right beneath her body. The sound of soft, even breathing cut through the air, reminding her that she wasn't alone.

Cat had to use the bathroom, but didn't want to go in that sterile white one, so she tiptoed past Tamsin's bed and let herself into the hall. Walking quickly, she reached the cozy blue bathroom by the back door.

When she came out, she eyed the door to Archie's office. What if she just stepped in there to check her email? If Officer Lamb had read her message, then he'd surely sent a reply. She suddenly yearned to read his words, to see what he told her to do.

Twisting the knob, she found the door open and walked inside. The computer's dark screen watched her approach, the chair turned slightly toward her as if patiently waiting for her to sit down.

Cat opened her email and began reading Officer Lamb's message, touched at his concern for her safety. She knew he'd understand. She was especially glad to find some lines about Quigley. But when she reached the end, she frowned. Why had he stopped in the middle of a word?

Did John Lamb know Cat was certain she'd met Quigley in her dream? He hadn't been a dream dog, it was really him. If Officer Lamb knew that, then could he be a visionary, too?

But even as she thought it, Cat knew it wasn't so. John Lamb was simply someone who cared about her. Perhaps he was the only person in the world who did. Caring people were in very short supply in her life.

"Thank you for writing back," Cat typed. *"I am not being hurt, but I am scared I might get turned out if Tamsin doesn't get well. I don't think Uncle Archie would do it, but he travels a lot, and sometimes Aunt Marlow gets a funny*

*look on her face when I catch her watching me. She looks
as if she's seeing a rat that accidentally got into her house.
Last night she made me brush Tamsin's hair even though I
was so tired I could barely keep my eyes open. But she
feeds me, and I have a bed to sleep on in Tamsin's room."*

Cat didn't add that she was happier sleeping on the
couch in the office.

*"I think it'll be better when Uncle Archie gets back, but
I'm not sure when that is. How's your heart? Mine's better
since I read your message."*

Cat pushed "send," then logged out of her account. She
slid off the desk chair and looked around the wood paneled
office, at the inviting dark leather couch with its memories
of Uncle Archie and Barrett, its wide cushions and tasseled
throw tossed over the back. Then she sank down onto the
couch and tugged the blanket over her. Settling into leather
that returned her body warmth, she drifted back to sleep.

Chapter 12

When she woke up, Cat went to the window and pushed the heavy drapes aside just enough to see dawn coloring the sky pink. Perhaps she should sneak back into Tamsin's room before anyone else woke up. Aunt Marlow hadn't forbidden her to sleep in the office, but she was pretty sure she wouldn't like it.

When Cat started down the hallway, a creeping sense of dread rose up and dogged her heels. What was causing it? She tried to focus, to figure out what it was that made her uneasy. Was Tamsin doing worse? Was she dead? Or had something happened to someone else in the house? She couldn't tell.

Hearing a noise in the kitchen, she carefully peered around the corner to see Barrett sitting at the table with a bowl of sugared cereal in front of him. Raising his head at the same time he raised his spoon, he didn't seem to notice the drips of milk falling back into his bowl. Smiling at Cat, he said, "Hi!" and then stood and walked toward her with open arms. She met him with a hug of her own, enjoying the warm envelope of love.

"Good morning," she mumbled into his shirt.

Barrett returned to his chair and Cat sat down opposite him, aware of the innocent pulse of white energy around his body. Yet beyond the white aura, a darker energy spread out around him like some kind of evil pressing in, trying to take over his whiteness like a disease.

"Do you want some cereal?" Barry asked, swinging his spoon toward a box that sported the picture of a colorful circus tent and a grinning clown wearing a pointy hat.

"What kind?"

"Circus Circles. See all the different colors?"

"They look good. I'll try some."

Barrett jumped up and got a bowl and spoon for Cat. He tipped the cereal box, letting the circles clatter into her bowl before pouring her a generous portion of milk.

As Cat she tapped the cereal down into its little lake of milk with the back of her spoon, Barrett said, "I'm glad you came."

"Thanks."

"You give good hugs."

"So do you." Cat took a bite of sweet cereal, surprised to find that the circles had different flavors.

"Good, huh?"

"Pretty good," Cat mumbled, then swallowed. "What are you doing today, Barrett?"

Barrett's face brightened. "I'm going to the city."

"New York City?"

Barrett nodded, crunching through another spoonful of his breakfast.

"By yourself?"

Barrett swallowed. "I've done it before. I've got a pass. I know where to get on the bus and where to get off. I like going different places. His face lit up with sudden joy. "There's a circus coming. Do you like circuses?"

Cat shrugged. "I've never been."

Barrett's smile slid into a little circle of surprise as round as his eyes. "You've never been to see the horseback riding ladies, or the marching elephants, or the clowns, or flying trapeze acrobats?"

"No."

"You've got to go!" Barrett cried. "You'll love it."

"Maybe when it gets here we can go together." Cat put her spoon down. "What about if you stay home today and we play a game?"

"Do you play Mousetrap?"

Cat's brow furrowed. "Gran sometimes set mousetraps at home when they'd get into the pantry, but I've never played a game called that."

Barrett laughed, covering his mouth with his big hand. "I'll show you." He walked out of sight down the hall, then returned with a rectangular box the size of two Circus Circles cereal boxes stuck together. On top was a cartoon of a colorful contraption with a cage poised over a sweating cartoon mouse. "This is the Mousetrap game. If the cage falls on your mouse, then you lose. If it falls on my mouse, then I lose."

"Sounds fun."

"Catriona!" Marlow called from down the hall, her voice tight with barely controlled anger. "Where are you?"

Cat froze as the air vibrated around her with hostile energy.

"She's eating breakfast," Barrett answered for Cat. Then he leaned forward and whispered, "She doesn't like Circus Circles. She thinks I should eat bran instead." He made a face. "If she'd eat Circus Circles, maybe she'd be happier."

Marlow swept into the kitchen, her silky coral-colored dressing gown billowing behind her. "You were not in Tamsin's room this morning," she said, her jaw tight. "She woke up and you were gone."

"I had to use the bathroom."

"You weren't in her bathroom." The words were short, like staccato notes.

"I didn't want to mess it up." Cat picked up her spoon and twirled it once in her fingers. "It's so white."

Marlow folded her arms. "We gave you a perfectly good place to sleep with a lovely bathroom attached." She offered a thin smile. "That's what family does. They are there for one another when needed." She hammered her last words home. "You need to be there for Tamsin."

"We were going to play a Mousetrap game." Cat turned to Barrett. "We can set it up in Tamsin's room, and she can play with us."

Barrett's eyes lit up with joy. "Absolutely!"

Marlow cut in, "That's not what Tamsin likes."

"But, Mother, she played it before."

"It's a child's game."

Barrett's mouth turned up in a hopeful smile. "Dad plays it with me."

Marlow's hands dropped to her sides. "He would." She turned her gaze on Cat. "Now you come back to Tamsin's room and spend some time with her. You can give her a manicure."

Cat's heart sank. "I've never done a manicure."

Marlow put out her hand toward Cat as if she to lead her to Tamsin's room. "She'll show you. She can teach you just how she likes it done."

"I only have a few more bites," Cat said, indicating her bowl. "I'll be there in a minute."

Marlow studied Cat for a long moment, then said, "All right. Be quick, and be sure to put your bowl in the sink." Then she turned and marched down the hallway.

Cat leaned forward, her eyes on Barrett. "Look, Barrett, I'll go do Tamsin's manicure, then we'll play Mousetrap, okay? Can you just set it up on the table?"

Barrett shook his head. "Mom doesn't like me to play in the kitchen. Dad and I play in his office." He got a conspiratorial grin on his face. "Sometimes we watch 'Dumbo' while we play. I like 'Dumbo,' even though it makes me cry." His gaze flitted to the window, and his voice filled with longing. "In the end, Dumbo finds friends."

Cat nodded. "Okay, set it up in there. I'll be as quick as I can. Then we'll have some fun, because I've never watched 'Dumbo'."

Barrett's eyes went wide. "Boy, oh, boy! Then it'll be like I'm watching it for the first time, too!" His eyes suddenly lost their spark. "I wish Tam would play with us. She used to watch 'Dumbo' with me when we were little."

"I'll ask her," Cat whispered. "Maybe she'll say 'yes!'"

Barrett nodded eagerly. "Absolutely."

"Okay, I'll see you soon."

Cat scooped more cereal into her mouth. When she finally stood up, Barrett said, "I'll take your bowl. I won't tell Mother I did. It will be our secret."

"Thanks," Cat mumbled through her last mouthful of cereal. Then she walked down the hall and knocked on Tamsin's closed door.

"Come in," Marlow called.

Cat walked in to see Tamsin sitting up against her pillows, her face pale against the deep rose of her nightgown, her slender hands resting on a plastic sheet laid over a yellow towel. Marlow had set out a bottle of nail polish remover, cotton balls, and various metal and wooden implements that were pointy, rounded, and rough. Cat shuddered inwardly, as if she'd stepped into a doctor's office, or a torturer's chamber.

"Come sit here," Marlow said, pointing to a chair next to the bed. "I'm going to get dressed. You listen to Tamsin and do exactly as she says. Understand?"

Cat nodded beneath her aunt's stern gaze. As Aunt Marlow headed toward the door, Tamsin asked, "Have you really never had a manicure?"

Cat shook her head.

"Have you ever worn nail polish?"

Cat shook her head. "But Gran used it all the time. She put some on me once, but I didn't like it." With a little tweak of sorrow, Cat added, "You would have liked her."

"Well, if you watched her do polish, then you probably know that first of all, you get a cotton ball wet with the nail polish remover, then rub it on my fingernails to take off the old polish." Tamsin wiggled her fingers. The nails seemed to have a perfectly smooth coat of pale pink color. Cat couldn't see a single problem with them, but she went ahead and did as she was directed. "Tell me about Gran," Tamsin said as Cat clumsily swiped at her fingernails, wrinkling her nose at the fumes from the nail polish remover.

Describing Gran helped Cat endure filing Tamsin's nails with a thin metal file and pushing down her perfect cuticles with a slender angled wooden stick. She told of how Gran liked to wear trousers and colorful buttoned up shirts, and how she liked to eat hot cereal with brown sugar and milk after sleeping in until 8:00 a.m.

"That's not sleeping in," Tamsin scoffed.

Cat's eyebrows rose. "I was up by six at the latest, but usually by five in the morning."

Tamsin's eyes narrowed. "Why?"

"To go out walking without running into people."

Tamsin cocked her head. "You're an odd one, aren't you?"

Cat did not bother answering the question, but her heart raced at being called "odd" yet again. She bent over Tamsin's hand, wishing she had her colorful hat on. She'd pull it down over her ears to block out her cousin's thoughtless words.

Staring at Tamsin's nails, Cat asked, "Now what?"

Tamsin glanced at a dizzying display of nail polish colors spread out on her dresser. There was every color Cat could imagine, as well as metallics such as gold, silver, and bronze. Focusing on a bottle of pale peach that appeared to match Tamsin's skin exactly, Cat reached for it.

"I feel like wearing Red Ribbons today," Tamsin said.

Cat had to sort through several bottles of red polish before she found the right one. Tensing, she tried to steady her hand as she applied the liquid to her cousin's nails.

With her head on her pillow and her eyes closed, Tamsin didn't notice the polish pooling at the base of her fingernails and edging up onto the skin at the sides in uneven smears until it looked like she'd tried to claw her way out of a cave.

The bedroom door suddenly opened and Barrett stuck his head inside. "Do you want to play with us, Tam?"

"You're supposed to knock!" Tamsin shouted, lifting her head from the pillow and opening her eyes.

Barrett's hopeful smile never wavered as he knocked on the open door, then shot his fist out and walked toward his sister. "What are you doing?" Tamsin asked, eyes wide with worry.

"Just giving you knuckles."

Cat made a fist and tapped Barrett's knuckles. "Like this," she said.

"Absolutely," Barrett said, angling his fist toward his sister.

"What's the point?" Tamsin asked.

"It's a way to say, 'hello,'" Cat said as Barrett dropped his hand and retreated back to the door. "We're going to play Mousetrap while we watch Dumbo," she added as she struggled to finish the thumbnail, the most awkward nail to paint because it was wider than the rest and sat rather sideways on the hand. "I've never done either one before."

Tamsin stared at her. "Did you even have electricity at your Gran's?"

Cat gave a short laugh which made her hand unsteady, swiping a bit of nail polish up on Tamsin's thumb toward her knuckle. "She was your Gran, too, and of course we had electricity."

Tamsin frowned. "It doesn't seem like you had anything. I can't play a game, anyway. It will mess up my nail polish."

"Well, I'm done," Cat said, twisting the lid on the nail polish bottle with relief. "I'm ready to play."

Tamsin stared at her fingernails. "What a mess! You've got to fix the mistakes."

Cat sagged. "I'll get better as I practice. Barrett and I want to play, so can't I do it later?"

With her fingers spread apart, Tamsin gestured at a glass jar of little cotton-tipped sticks. "No. Do it now. Just dip one of those in nail polish remover, then clean up around my fingernails. If you rub some off my nail, you'll have to put more polish on, though." She examined her nails more closely. "You're really not very good at this."

"Remember, Tam, we all have different talents," Barrett said from the doorway.

Tamsin's eyes narrowed. "What do you know about it? You don't have any."

Startled at Tamsin's unkind words, Cat glanced up, recognizing sorrow and jealousy behind the scowl on her cousin's tragically beautiful face. Was she jealous that Barrett was healthy and she was not?

To Cat's surprise, Barrett laughed as if Tamsin couldn't be serious. "If you only knew." He twisted his hand, turning the doorknob, and then released it to roll back again. "Please let me hug you. I have a talent for hugging, you know."

Tamsin waved her fingers at him in exaggerated circles. "Duh. I don't want you messing up my manicure." She took a closer look at her nails. "Even though it's pretty messy anyway."

"Here," Cat said, holding up a wet cotton stick, anxious to be done. "I'll try to fix it."

As she dabbed at the red polish on the skin of Tamsin's thumb, Barrett said, "You're too busy now, Cat. I'm going to ride the bus. We can play later."

Sudden sensations of blood and pain washed over Cat as she whirled to face Barrett, sliding the wet stick across Tamsin's nail. "No! Please, wait just a little longer. I'm almost done."

"Okay." Barrett shrugged, but didn't smile. "I'll get the movie set up." He disappeared, leaving the door open.

"He drives me crazy," Tamsin said, gazing at the open door.

"But you love him anyway."

Tamsin huffed, her eyes guarded, and Cat got busy cleaning up the red mess and reapplying polish to the thumbnail, wishing Tamsin had chosen the peach colored polish instead.

Chapter 13

As soon as Cat opened the office door, Barrett looked up from his place beside the Mousetrap game board, his face brightening. Behind him, the image of a colorful circus train waited on the TV screen, ready to start down the track. Barrett pushed the "play" button and the train chugged along to the accompaniment of bright circus music.

Cat settled herself in a chair beside Barrett's and gazed in wonder at a game made of colorful little plastic scaffolds, a bathtub, a little molded shoe on the end of a thin pole, a bucket, and a semi-spherical cage. Barrett handed her a die. "You go first. Move your mouse the number of spaces that you roll, from one to six. What color of mouse do you want?"

They were on their third turn when Marlow called, "Catriona!"

Cat jumped, her hand poised over her red plastic mouse. "Does she mind if we play in here?" she whispered to Barrett.

"I don't think so," Barrett answered, fitting a piece of the structure together on the game board. "Dad doesn't mind, so why should she?"

"I'm in the office," Cat called.

Swift footfalls approached the doorway before Marlow appeared. "What is going on?"

"We're playing," Barrett said. "Do you want to play, too? We could start over. We'll even start Dumbo at the beginning. You don't mind, do you Cat?"

"No," Marlow said. "I don't want to play, and neither does Cat. She has other things to do."

With her fingers still on her mouse, Cat said, "I finished Tamsin's nails."

"That's not all she needs done. She needs her hair brushed, her clothes hung up, and most of all she needs someone to talk to. Can you imagine what it's like to lie in bed all day?" Marlow spoke more slowly, emphasizing her words, "You need to spend time with her."

"We asked her to play with us," Barrett said, rolling the die. "We were going to set up the game in her room, but she said 'no.'"

"Of course she did." Marlow flicked her hand toward the game board. "She wants to do more meaningful things than play a child's game. Come along, Cat."

"I'd like to finish the game first."

"No. You never should have started it. Barrett can go do something else."

Cat shot a look at her cousin, whose smile sagged as he dismantled the apparatus he'd just set up. "Don't leave," she whispered to him, trying not to panic. Barrett only shrugged, but the determined gleam in his eye made Cat afraid. She didn't want him to go, but she couldn't think of anything else to say. She follow Marlow to Tamsin's room.

Just before walking through Tamsin's door, Cat said, "Barrett shouldn't leave the house."

Marlow gave her a frosty glance. "Barrett is perfectly capable of maneuvering the New Jersey Transit system. He may… take a little longer to learn some things, but he's not incompetent."

Cat tried to speak calmly. "I'm afraid something will happen to him."

Marlow's gaze sharpened. "Are you having a vision? Do you see anything about Tamsin?"

Startled by her aunt's fervor, Cat stepped back, bumping into the wall. "It's nothing clear. It's just a feeling, and it's about Barrett. He's going to get hurt."

Marlow waved her hand. "That happens all the time. He's a boy, after all. Boys are always rowdy."

"It feels worse than that." Cat tried to keep her tears under control.

"Well, don't worry, I'll go have a talk with him and tell him to be extra careful today. Now take your mind off Barrett and go in there to make something good happen for Tamsin."

"I can't make things happen."

Marlow smiled. "Just try."

Cat sat by Tamsin's bed and practiced braiding her hair. At midday, Marlow brought them golden brown grilled cheese sandwiches on fine white china, accompanied by a white sauce speckled with green and brown bits. A colorful salad of orange, green, and red vegetables with purple grapes sat on the side of the plate in a white bowl.

When her mother left the room, Tamsin dipped her sandwich in her sauce and took a bite, so Cat did the same. Even though it was delicious, it was hard to enjoy her food with her thoughts flitting to Barrett and the darkness she'd seen around him.

Tamsin sighed and put her partially eaten sandwich on the side of her plate. "I'm really hungry for chili cheese fries."

"I'll tell Aunt Marlow."

Tamsin let out an impatient huff of air. "She won't let me have them." Her voice changed to a mockery of her mother's voice. "They're too messy."

Cat licked a bit of errant white sauce off her finger. "Not if you eat them with a fork."

Tamsin gave her a suspicious look. "Are you serious?"

Cat shrugged. "Why not?"

Tamsin gave a little half smile. "Why not, indeed?"

After lunch, Tamsin made Cat tell stories about castles and princesses. Cat didn't know any stories like that besides Cinderella, but Tamsin ordered her to make one up. "Here's what we'll do," Cat said. "I'll start a story, then when I stop, you tell the next part."

"But I don't know what's going to happen!"

"You can say anything," Cat explained. "Even one thing, such as a mouse ran across the floor. Then if you don't want to add any more, I'll take up the story again." When Tamsin looked doubtful, Cat said, "Let's just give it a go."

After a couple of tentative tries, Tamsin became a willing participant in creating a whimsical story about a princess who carried her bed about on her back, using it as a sailboat and a sled and a flying machine to see the world.

When Marlow checked on them, she smiled at the sight of Cat sitting beside Tamsin's bed while Tamsin created an animated story segment about the princess riding the ferris wheel at a circus.

The next time Marlow checked on the girls, she announced, "Dinner's in an hour. Do you need anything?"

"I need a bathroom break," Cat said, standing. "I'm going down the hall to stretch my legs."

"Come right back," Tamsin said, a touch of pleading in her voice.

As soon as she was in the hall with Marlow, Cat asked, "Have you heard from Barrett?"

"No, but I told him to be careful."

Cat squeezed her hands together. "I'm worried about him."

"Then you're worried about the wrong person. If you don't focus on Tamsin, then you aren't doing your part for this family. Do you understand your responsibilities?"

When Cat looked up at her aunt, her focus shifted without conscious control, changing her aunt's angry eyes into ones pouring rivers of tears down her cheeks as she cried over her dead daughter. There was no way to stop it. It would happen. When it did, would Marlow blame her? Perhaps it would be better to get kicked out of the house before Tamsin died. If Cat was on her own, she may find some way to get home to England. Perhaps she could offer to work on the ship or something.

"Do you understand?"

Before Cat could reply, the kitchen door slammed and someone fell heavily into a chair with a loud moan. Cat dashed past Marlow, reaching the kitchen first. Barrett sat at the table with a crumpled paper bag held against his head in a vain attempt to stop a trail of blood from trickling down his face. Fresh blood streaked his neck and hands.

"Barrett!" Marlow cried. "You're bleeding!"

"At least I'm not dead," Barrett mumbled.

While Cat tugged on the paper bag to try to get a look at the wound, Marlow put a hand out and touched Barrett's hair. Startled, he jerked his head, and she drew back. "My goodness, why didn't you come in the back door by the bathroom where we could get you cleaned up right away?" Marlow headed for the broom closet where she kept rags, while Cat dashed for the kitchen drawer full of fluffy, clean dishtowels. Cat yanked one out and hurried to Barrett's side, gently removing the paper bag to reveal an ugly gash. She covered it with the towel, pressing against the wound.

Marlow reappeared, holding out a threadbare cleaning rag. When she saw Cat tending to Barrett, she stopped and stared. Whether concentrating on the blood dotting the table, at her son's wound, or the dishtowel turning red, Cat wasn't sure.

"Come on, let's wash you off at the sink," Cat said.

Barrett stood and followed Cat, his face uncharacteristically solemn. "Why did they hurt me again?"

Tamsin's voice sounded from down the hall. "You've got to stop annoying them. You're the ugly duckling trying to fit in, and you just don't."

"She doesn't mean that," Barrett said as Cat turned on the faucet. Sticking his hands under the running water, he watched it turn pink and swirl down the drain.

With the dishtowel removed, Cat noticed fresh blood swelling to spill down the side of his head again. Grabbing a fresh towel to hold against the wound, Cat dampened a clean corner of the bloody one to dab at the blood running down Barrett's face and neck. "He needs a doctor," she called.

"Is it that bad?" Marlow asked, standing back as if afraid Barrett was contagious.

Annoyed, Cat glanced over her shoulder at Barrett's mother, the woman who was supposed to be doing all the things Cat was doing. She saw Marlow biting her lip, lipstick staining the very edge of her teeth, while fear of losing her son welled up fresh and horrible to twine with her familiar fear of losing her daughter. The jumble of terror hammered at her heart, creating such pain she could scarcely move.

"Marlow, you must drive him to hospital," Cat snapped. "You are the only one with a driving license. Step on it!"

The unbending steel of Cat's voice seemed to break through Marlow's shell. She leapt into action, hurrying to the pantry and pulling out a box of large garbage bags, calling, "Bring him to the car." Marlow grabbed the car key by the door and hurried out to the garage.

Cat turned off the water and walked Barret out to the car where Marlow was placing garbage bags over the passenger seat. "You stay here with Tamsin," Marlow said as Cat made sure that Barrett was buckled in securely against the crackly plastic bags.

"I will."

After the car drove away, Cat returned to Tamsin's room and stood in the doorway.

"What did he do this time?" Tamsin asked.

"His head is badly cut."

Tamsin examined her fingernails. "He should be more careful."

After a moment, Cat asked, "Why don't you like your brother?"

Tamsin put her hands up in surrender. "Isn't it obvious? He's hard to talk to. In case you haven't noticed, he has never grown up. He doesn't understand half of what I say. He's just so annoying."

"I would have loved to have a brother or sister."

Tamsin snorted. "You can have mine."

Cat walked over and sat in the chair by the bed. "What did you think of him when you were little?"

Tamsin shrugged. "He was fun to play with, I guess. Sometimes we played with trucks, sometimes with dolls. But now things are…different."

Cat shivered and rubbed her hands along her arms. "You never know when you're going to lose someone. When they're gone, you can't get them back to make things right."

Tamsin shrugged. "I don't see anything wrong."

After a moment's silence, Cat scooted her chair closer to the bed. "What's one thing you like about him right now?"

Tamsin frowned.

"Just one."

Tamsin's eyes wandered to the wall, where a color print hung, showing a mother and daughter walking away through a meadow side by side in long dresses. "He's always smiling."

"He wasn't too happy just now."

"Well," Tamsin shrugged and placed her hands, one over the other, on top of her comforter. "I suppose that nothing lasts forever." She yawned.

"Do you want to sleep?"

"First I need to use the bathroom." Tamsin struggled to sit up and get her legs over the side of the bed. They were alarmingly thin, like young willow branches. How could they possibly support her weight, as slight as it was?

"Do you need help?" Cat asked.

Tamsin glanced at Cat. "The day I need help to wipe my bum is a day I won't survive."

Cat lowered her eyes, but from her peripheral vision she saw her cousin grab her walker and shuffle awkwardly into the bathroom, grunting with effort. Then the bathroom door closed behind her.

With no one to stop her, Cat hurried to the office and slid into the computer chair. Typing frantically, she brought up her email to find not only a reply from John Lamb, but also a message from Mrs. Kane. She opened Sarah Kane's message first.

"Cat, I hope you're alright. I would have brought you with us if I could. Is America as odd as Australia? The animals here are so strange, and water goes down the drain backwards, if you can believe it. It's enough to make my eyes cross. Richard is talking of extending our holiday. Enough about me. I hope you're having a wonderful time, getting to know your lovely auntie and your cousins. Love you, dear."

Cat couldn't bring herself to tell Sarah Kane how unhappy she was, so she replied with a description of Tamsin's lovely room, their fingernail painting parties, and eating Circus Circles with Barrett. She ended with,

"Try making friends with a kangaroo. Maybe they just seem odd because you don't know them yet."

Then Cat opened John Lamb's message.

"It sounds as if I need to give Marlow Davies a call. I'll say it's a routine check and see what I can get from her. Just so you know, at night Quigley always circles until he finally lies down with his head facing toward the United States. It's as if he knows you're there. In the meantime, do the best you can while we look into things."

Puzzled, Cat wondered how Officer Lamb would know how Quigley slept. She typed,

"When you call, remember the time difference. I still get sleepy earlier than anyone else. I really like Barrett, but I'm worried because he came home bleeding today and asked why they always hurt him. I don't know who "they" are, and Aunt Marlow didn't seem keen on taking him to a doctor, but I said she should. I'm waiting for them to come back, but then I can't send messages because she wants me to stay in Tamsin's room all the time. I'm getting on better with Tamsin. How did you know about Quigley sleeping? Did Charlie tell you? You forgot to let me know how your heart is doing. Don't forget next time or I'll have to fly over and see for myself. Do you remember telling me your mother's maiden name is 'Lyon?' I could use a lion's heart right now. Love, Cat."

As soon as she pushed "send," a screech sounded down the hallway, "Where are you? You're not supposed to leave me. I'm telling Mother!"

Chapter 14

When she rounded the doorway, Catriona was surprised to see Tamsin grabbing onto her doorjamb with one hand and her walker with the other. Her face was alarmingly contorted, more from fear than anger.

"You need to get back to bed." Cat took her cousin's thin arm, wondering if it might break from her touch.

"You shouldn't leave me," Tamsin said, breathless.

"Why? You've been alone before."

"Mother says you need to stay with me or I'll die."

"That's not so. Come on." Cat helped Tamsin back to her bed.

"Why would Mother say it if it's not true?" Tamsin asked, her delicate jaw thrust out in defiance.

Cat sat down and tried to hold Tamsin's hand, but she pulled it back, her wild eyes darting from Cat to the door and then back again. "Why aren't you curing me? Mother said you would."

"She shouldn't have." Cat rubbed her forehead.

Tamsin's beautiful eyes narrowed. "You just don't want to cure me. You don't even like me, do you? You think I'm weird. You think you're superior, because I'm sick and can hardly walk."

Cat squeezed her hands together, wanting to reach out and comfort Tamsin, but afraid that her touch would only annoy her more.

Tamsin shook her head, then squinched her face up as if in pain.

"Are you alright?"

"What do you care?" Tamsin pointed a shaking finger at her dressing table where her brush, comb, pins, and a laptop sat. "Find me a new hairstyle."

Cat stood, picked up the brush, and slid her fingers beneath Tamsin's hair. Her cousin rolled her head across the pillow in an effort to pull away. "Not that," she snapped. "Go online and find some styles. I'll tell you which ones I want."

Even though Tamsin's eyelids drooped, Cat obediently pulled up some hairstyles. Four awkward style attempts later, the sound of the door opening made both girls pause.

Marlow came into the room, her face brightening when she saw Cat standing behind Tamsin with a hairbrush in her hand and pins bristling from the corner of her mouth. "Well, it looks like you two have used your time well." Marlow sat on the edge of Tamsin's bed while Barrett edged around the doorway, revealing a white bandage wrapped around his head. Cat almost didn't recognize him without his smile. He took in Marlow and Tamsin sitting side by side, their heads nearly touching, before slipping out of sight.

Cat put down the hairbrush, spit out the pins, and headed for the door.

"Where are you going?" Marlow demanded.

"I just want to check on Barrett."

"Barrett has just been seen by a doctor. Are you a doctor?"

"No."

"Then there's nothing you can do for him. Come back here. You are to stay in Tamsin's room with her, use her bathroom, and sleep in that bed." Marlow pointed to the twin bed pressed tightly against the wall. "No more nonsense." Her voice rose to a near hysteric pitch. "Just do what you came here to do before it's too late!"

Even Tamsin seemed cowed by her mother's words, her frightened eyes sliding from Marlow to Cat and back again.

"Alright," Cat said, drawing herself up to her full height, which wasn't much, but it was all she had. "I'll go to bed in this room."

It wasn't a lie. But what she would do after she went to bed remained to be seen.

Chapter 15

Cat heard movement over the sound of Tamsin's shallow, even breaths. Turning her head, Cat saw that Tamsin was asleep. She listened intently. There it was again, coming from the hallway. A soft rustle. A careful foot fall.

Pushing back her covers, Cat got up and crept to the doorway. Pausing for a moment, she wondered if Marlow was out there, checking up on her. Then she heard a faint grunt that didn't sound like her aunt. Pushing the door open, she nearly hit Barrett in the back.

"Hey!" Barrett cried.

"Shhh, you'll wake your mother."

"Not likely. She listens to nighttime talks while she sleeps. They're supposed to make her rich and beautiful." He hitched the straps of a rucksack up on his shoulders.

"What are you doing?" Cat asked, even though she already knew.

"Leaving." Barrett walked toward the back door.

"Why?"

He put his hand on the doorknob. "I'm going to find some nice people, ones who like smiles and hugs, and live with them."

Cat tiptoed after Barrett and took hold of his arm. "Hold on. Listen to me. I was really sad to leave my home. In your home, you have a bed, food, and people who care about you, even if they don't say so. What will you eat out there? Where will you sleep?" Cat pointed to Barry's bandage. "Who will be your friend when you get hurt?"

Barrett's gaze grew crafty. Then he bent down and said in a loud whisper, "I'm going to join the circus!"

Cat hadn't seen this coming. Where was her visionary talent when she wanted it? Stalling for time, she asked, "How far is that?"

"Mahwah."

"How do you know they'd take you?"

"They'll take me because I'm strong. I can help set up the tents. I'll even shovel animal poop." When Cat didn't reply, Barrett insisted, "I would. I would do that so I could stay."

"I believe you," Cat said, thinking hard. If Barrett left on his own, there was no telling what might happen to him. She thought about waking up Aunt Marlow, but it didn't feel right. The way Marlow treated her son's injury made Cat uneasy. How would she react to him running away? Cat could not imagine a good ending to this situation.

Then a sudden thought struck her. There was no compelling reason for her to stay here, either. She couldn't cure Tamsin like her aunt expected. If Cat was gone, Marlow couldn't insist that she braid Tamsin's hair, do her nails, or sit in her room for hours on end. If Cat left with Barrett, she could watch over him, and call for help in case of emergency.

But shouldn't she stay until Uncle Archie got back? He seemed nice enough. But when would he return? Cat's mind tingled with the feeling that even when Archie was home, he wasn't really here.

The more Cat imagined being out from under Marlow's thumb and beyond range of her accusing, desperate gaze, the more she liked it.

"May I come with you?" she asked.

Barrett's gaze captured hers in the dim hall light. "You want to join the circus?" Barrett sounded hopeful.

"I don't know if I'm good enough, but I want to go with you," Cat said.

Barrett's face split into a smile. "Absolutely!" He punched a fist out in front of him, and Cat tapped it with her knuckles.

"We must be quite," Cat reminded him.

He grinned and whispered, "Maybe we could be clowns

together. Wouldn't that be fun?"

"We'll see. Hang on now 'til I get my things."

"I'll wait outside," Barrett said, pulling open the door.

"Promise you won't leave without me?"

"Promise."

Tamsin didn't wake when Cat pulled on her shoes and grabbed her clothes, carrying them out into the hall with her before stuffing them into her rucksack. As soon as she stepped outside, she pulled on her hat with the little bells.

"I like your hat," Barrett said.

"Thanks." Cat gave her head a shake, sending the bells jingling softly, which made Barrett laugh.

In minutes, the cousins were walking down the street, the packs on their backs casting strange shadows that first followed, then slid ahead to lead the way as the streetlights passed over their heads. The further they got from the house, the happier Barrett became. He never complained about Cat's need to take two steps to every one of his as he ambled along beside her, talking about the circus. It was surprising how much he knew about its inner workings.

As she gazed at her cousin gesturing with his big hands while talking about the different acts, the people who performed them, and the proper care of circus animals, Cat's insight increased. She saw his bright aura expand even further around him as he spoke with joy of being around kind people and animals. She realized she was walking beside a gentle giant, a soldier, a savior.

Barrett remained blissfully unaware of the dark shroud curved over his halo of bright light. There was something out there that meant to harm him, and Cat resolved to stay close enough to help deflect any tragedy.

They didn't wait long at the bus stop, and when they boarded, none of the half dozen sleepy passengers gave them a second glance. Cat sat on the edge of her seat, looking out into the dark night punctuated by hard bits of light from streetlights, buildings, and traffic lights.

When they reached Seacaucus Junction, they got off the bus. Cat held tightly to her rucksack straps, unsure of where to go. Barrett put his arm around her, leading her unerringly to their connecting bus. Once they found a seat, Cat sank back onto the upholstery with a sigh, grateful to have Barrett sitting so warm and solid beside her.

Cat woke suddenly when the bus slowed to a stop. Lifting her head from Barrett's shoulder, she gazed out onto Mahwah's bus terminal. "Come on," Barrett said, standing in the aisle, hand extended. Cat took it and followed him out onto the street.

As they walked in the early morning light, Cat kept staring at New York City's skyscrapers on the horizon, then gasped in delight when the sun rose, washing the city in a warm glow.

Barrett let go of Cat's hand, slung his pack around by one strap, and fumbled inside until he pulled out a dented box of Circus Circles. "Hungry?"he asked, holding it out toward Cat.

Cat took a handful and chewed on the cereal as she walked. Barrett helped himself to a handful before explaining, "I didn't know how to bring any milk." He pushed the cereal into his mouth and crunched happily. After swallowing, he added, "I brought some little bottles of juice."

"Good thinking."

Their cold breakfast didn't last as long as their search for the circus. Cat was growing hungry again as she wondered if they'd already passed a landmark or two, but everything was so new, she could have been wrong. Barrett plucked at his head bandage as he glanced from side to side, his smile fading into an expression of intense concentration.

Trying to make him leave his bandage alone, Cat asked, "Will you hold my hand?"

Barrett willingly took her hand, but continued to tug on his bandage periodically with his other hand.

Finally, Cat asked, "Do you want to wear this?" She stopped and pulled her yarn hat off her head, bells jingling faintly.

"Absolutely," Barrett said. As he reached for the hat, Cat saw that his bandage was already loose. Barrett pulled the hat on over the bandage, then swung his head from side to side, feeling the dangling bells swish across his face and neck. "I like it," he said with a grin.

Cat was wishing mightily that they had something more substantial to eat when a striped circus tent came into view. "There it is," Barrett shouted with delight, "the Curious Circus!" Yanking off the hat pulled his bandage loose. When he tossed the hat back to Cat, the bandage tumbled to the ground. With just a stained gauze pad taped to his head, Barrett grabbed Cat's hand and pulled her along with him so fast, it was all she could do to keep hold of the hat as her legs hurried to keep up.

When they reached the circus grounds, Barrett slowed. Cat let go of his hand to pull on her hat, feeling safer with it on in this strange place. People were busy all around them, setting things up, exercising animals, and moving between obstacles with purpose. A long tent set up next to a big trailer gave off the tantalizing aroma of chicken and hamburgers. Cat sniffed, hoping they might be able to buy some food. She wondered if Barrett had any money, because she didn't.

With her gaze focused on the mess tent, she didn't notice anyone in their path until Barrett jerked to a sudden stop and a deep, angry voice yelled, "Dumkopf!"

Startled, Cat turned to see a thickly built, bald-headed man with scars crisscrossing his scalp. Even though Barrett was fairly tall, this man was a giant, with muscles bulging beneath his shirt sleeves.

Barrett's face broke into a delighted smile. "You're the strong man, one of the most important performers! Would you please show me how to lift weights? I'll be your workout partner."

When the strong man's gaze slid down to the red birthmark on Barrett's neck, his expression changed from anger to horror. A wall of hopelessness slammed from him into Cat so forcefully that she stumbled backward. "Are you crazy?" he roared. "What are you really wanting?"

Barrett shot his fist out toward the giant, who stepped back, mouth open as if getting ready to scream.

"He just wants to tap your knuckles," Cat explained, trying to keep things calm. "It's his way of shaking hands."

"I do not touch." The man rubbed his hand over his scarred head, soul-deep sorrow swirling around him so thick that it made Cat want to cry. What had happened to this strong man that made him so weak? And what was it about Barrett's birthmark that disturbed him so much?

"Are you alright?" she asked.

The giant glared at her. "Why you asking? Something wrong with you?"

Cat shrank back while Barrett gave her a puzzled glance, then answered for her, "Nothing's wrong with her."

"Then why's she wearing ridiculous fruit salad hat?"

Cat pulled her colorful hat off, bells tinkling as she shoved it into her pocket.

"It's her circus hat," Barrett said. "We're joining the circus, so I'd like to be your friend."

Sensing that Barrett wanted to give the muscled man a hug, Cat grabbed her cousin's arm. Although she agreed that the fierce man could use a hug, it seemed to her it should have happened when he was small enough that his parents' arms could still reach around him. She was pretty sure he wouldn't accept one now.

Barrett glanced down at her, then back at the strong man. "I'm Barrett Davies. What's your name?"

"Gunther," the man growled in an accent that sounded as if he was clearing his throat.

"Gunther is a strong name," Barrett said. "Like 'Samson.'"

"Barrett is not strong," Gunther said, folding his muscled arms. It looked like a strain for him to get them to meet across his chest.

"Why?"

"It sounds like a man who sits by a fire with a cup of tea."

Barrett looked confused.

"Barry is a strong name."

Barrett turned to Cat with a broad smile. "My circus

name is Barry!"

"You can't join the circus," Gunther announced.

Barry's smile faltered, but he said, "I think we can."

"Did you make an application?"

"No."

"Did you talk to the ringmaster?"

"Not yet."

"You won't get hired."

"Oh, I will," Barry said, nodding earnestly. "Where's the ringmaster?"

"Could be in his trailer, or at lunch." Gunther's biceps bulged as he pushed a thumb back over his shoulder toward the tent with the delicious smells. "I wouldn't bother if I were you."

As Barry and Cat walked away, Gunther growled after them, "What do you think you and your little sister can do that is worthy of the circus?"

Barry turned around, beaming. "Anything!"

As they crossed the midway to the mess tent, they drew even with a petite woman whose long brown hair was clipped up on the back of her head so that the ends cascaded down like a horse's tail. When Barry saw the glossy white horse at the end of the woman's lead rope shaking its head, he stopped and asked in amazement, "Is that horse telling you 'no?'"

The woman turned, surprise plain on her her pretty face, which didn't look much older than Barry. "He is," she answered, "It's part of our act." Then she covered her mouth with her slender fingers. "But maybe I shouldn't have told you. It might spoil our performance."

Barry slid his finger across his chest first one way, then

the other. "I won't tell anyone. Cross my heart." Sticking his fist out, he stepped closer to the young lady. "My name's Barry. Just tap my knuckles with your fist."

She smiled and did as he said. "I'm Felicianna. My horse is Abby."

Barry touched the top of Cat's head. "This is Cat."

Felicianna tipped her head, and with a mischievous smile, asked, "Does that mean you like cats?"

"I actually have a dog."

Felicianna stroked Abby's nose. "I see. Are both of you animal lovers like me?"

"Absolutely!" Barry answered while Cat gave a little shrug. "I even love hyenas," Barry continued. "They make such a funny sound. Do you like them, too?"

"Of course," Felicianna answered."They have their place in the world."

"You have a good brain, and you're pretty, too," Barry said, his eyes full of admiration.

Felicianna gave a nod of acknowledgment, then glanced up at Barry. "You certainly say what you think, don't you?"

Barry spread his hands. "I don't know how else to talk."

Felicianna laughed. "The world would be a better place if more people spoke like you."

"I could teach them."

Cat's stomach growled so loudly that Barry glanced at her. "Sounds like the Circus Circles didn't last."

"Circus Circles?" Felicianna asked. "Is that your act?"

"It's cereal," Barry explained. "We had some for breakfast, but that was awhile ago."

"Oh." Feliciana glanced toward the exit. "I don't know of any place near here to eat."

"I do." Barry pointed to the mess tent.

"But that's for circus employees."

"Exactly. See you later, Felicianna. Bye, Abby."

The horse nodded as Barry and Cat moved away. Felicianna watched them go, her eyes full of warm curiosity. When Barry glanced back toward her, he nearly tripped over three little dark-haired men hurrying between the mess tent and a row of trailers.

"Hey!" one of them called. "Watch where you're going!"

Just as Barry turned to say, "Sorry," the three men tumbled and leaped until they stood on one another's shoulders. The uppermost man looked Barry in the eye, his swarthy face squinting in a challenge for right-of-way as sunlight glinted off his black hair.

"Wow!" Barry said, applauding the acrobats. "You guys are the best!"

The frowns on the little men's faces turned to looks of puzzlement. With his legs braced wide, the acrobat on the bottom gripped the legs of the man on his shoulders and called, "Are you going to punch him out or what?"

"Naw," said the guy on top. "He's cool." Jumping down to the ground, he tucked his head under and rolled himself up onto his feet. The second man flipped forward into a somersault and wound up standing, while the man on the bottom stretched his arms around behind him to press on the small of his back as he twisted from side to side.

Barry stuck his fist down toward the men. The man from the top of the human tower gave his fellows a sidelong glance.

"You're supposed to..." Cat began.

"I know what to do," the man said, bumping his fist against Barry's. Delighted, Barry moved his hand to the next man and the next as he said, "I'm Barry and this is Cat. Who are you?"

"I'm Eeny," said the man who'd been at the top of the stack. Pointing to the second man, he said, "That's Meeny." He ended by pointing at the bottom man, "and that's Miney." With both hands out at his sides, palms up, he finished with, "There ain't no mo'."

Barry laughed and Cat smiled.

"That joke is so old," said a man in a bright green suit as he strode past the newcomers, his thin body moving so fluidly that it looked like it was made of thin strands of cartilage instead of bone. Cat couldn't see his face, but his wavy brown hair was long enough to brush his shoulders.

"Oldie but goodie," Eeny defended himself, not sounding the least bit pleased as he watched the man disappear inside the mess tent.

"Who's that?" Barry asked.

"Bendo the Clown."

"A clown? He didn't seem very happy for a clown."

Meeny scuffed at the dirt with his size 3 foot. "He's sort of a clown acrobat. He can bend himself really small to fit into a suitcase for the other clowns to carry around as part of their act."

"What he's happiest bending is words," Miney said with a scowl.

"How do you bend words?" Barry asked.

"He makes what you say sound like what he wants it to mean, even if it's not the way you said it."

"Enough talk," Eeny said. "Come on guys, we've got to

practice. Let's go."

When Cat and Barry reached the mess tent, it was nearly empty. Bendo turned his narrow face toward them as they walked in, his thin lips pressed into a straight line. Two blond performers in sequins sat across a long folding table from a squat man whose face appeared squashed, like a troll that had survived a rock falling on him. Four cooks moved around behind the long serving table, scraping leftovers, sweeping, and stacking pans before carrying them into the trailer behind them.

Barry strode up to the serving table and addressed a dark skinned cook with thick, black tattoos swirling over every part of his visible skin. "Hello. I'm Barry." He didn't extend his fist, probably because the cook's hands were full of utensils. "I'm looking for the ringmaster."

"He's been and gone."

"Where might I find him now?"

The cook jabbed a serving spoon toward the tent opening. "In his trailer." The cook glanced at Cat and saw her eyeing the the potatoes clinging to the sides of the big rectangular pan in the warming tray. Voice softening, he asked, "Are you hungry?"

"Absolutely," Barry said.

Cat answered with a quiet, "Yes."

"I'm just going to toss these potatoes, unless you want them."

"Yes, please," Barry answered with a nod. "Cat and I will share. But we need to see the ringmaster first."

The cook tipped his head. "Cat, huh? You needn't be in such a hurry. He'll still be around after you eat."

Another cook, a red-haired lady with sparkly green

eyelids, stopped in front of the newcomers. "Do cats like chicken?" she asked with a quirk of her red lips.

"I do," Cat answered, her stomach nearly caved in from hunger. "Thank you."

Cat and Barry eventually sat down to plates loaded with potatoes, chicken, green beans, and rolls. Barry had chosen chocolate milk to drink, and Cat had taken a can of orange juice.

"See how good it is here?" Barry asked as he pushed his fork into the potatoes.

"You were right," Cat said.

"The people here don't think anyone is weird," Barry explained.

Bendo glided over to their table and slid his legs onto the bench so he could sit facing them. "Hello," he said, his pale blue eyes blinking above his pointed nose. "Have you run away to join the circus?"

Cat looked at Barry to see what he would say, but his mouth was full of food. When she turned back, she was startled to find Bendo's gaze on her, a wave of cautious curiosity rolling off him as he studied her face.

"Me?"

"Yes, you. Of course, since you're with your brother, we won't be calling the cops on you just yet." His face was serious, but his voice was playful.

Barry swallowed his mouthful and said, "We're here to see the ringmaster for a job."

"But does he want to see you?" Bendo asked, pointing a slender finger at Barry.

"Of course."

"Well, if you are determined, follow me. I'll take you to

him."

"I'm not finished yet," Cat said, pulling her tray a little closer.

"Then I shall return."

Bendo stood with admirable grace and strode back to the others. When he bent over the table and said something, the people laughed and turned to look at Barry and Cat. Barry waved at them.

"Don't you know they're laughing at us?" Cat asked, averting her gaze.

"They can't laugh at us if we laugh, too," Barry explained. "That makes them laugh with us."

As soon as they finished eating, they returned their trays and thanked the cooks again. Turning around, they nearly bumped into Bendo. "This way," he said, and led them to one of several circus trailers parked at the back of the lot. When he knocked, a voice like a megaphone boomed, "Come in!"

Bendo opened the door and made an elegant gesture for Barry and Cat to step inside. Barry led the way, with Cat right behind him. Bendo stayed outside, staring in as a man of about forty looked up from a table scattered with papers, file boxes, and a laptop computer. His round face looked questioningly from Bendo to Barry and Cat, then back again. That's when Bendo shut the door.

The man stood, revealing a square, muscular body with a rounded stomach. He stuck out his hand, "Manny Shaw, ringmaster. What can I do for you?"

Barry made a fist, but Cat caught it in her hand and shook her head. Barry uncurled his fingers and shook Manny's hand. "I'm Barry and this is Cat." He tipped his head toward Catriona.

"Any chance you two are incredibly mismatched twins?" Manny squinted at them with amusement, and Cat could almost see him formulating a headline for a new act.

"No," Barry answered, "but I wish we were."

"Family?"

"Yes."

When the ringmaster extended his hand toward Cat, she hesitated. Too many unsettling insights had come her way today. Would she get one from him, too? But she had to shake his hand if they were to have any chance of staying.

Bracing herself, she took hold of Manny's big hand. As soon as she did, warmth slid up her arm and spread out, filling her with a sensation of such complete acceptance that her knees went weak. She'd always had to work toward earning approval from others, even a bit with Gran, who remained puzzled about her abilities. No one had ever freely granted her complete acceptance until now. When Manny let go, Cat wanted to touch him again just to experience the wondrous sensation of feeling like she was perfectly fine just the way she was, with no expectation to change a single thing.

"What can I do for you?" Manny asked with a genial smile.

"We've come to work for you," Barry said.

"Is that so?" Manny glanced from one to the other. "Both of you?"

Barry nodded. "We're big fans." He tipped his head and recited, "Circus Circles are delicious and nutritious." Anyone else would think Barry was being ironic. Only Cat knew he was sincere.

"Well, then," Manny said, pinching his chin with his fingers. "What can you do?"

"Anything." Barry leaned forward, his hands splayed on the table. "We can feed or clean up after animals. I could move your tents, or get things for people. Cat can run errands, too. We could take tickets, sweep, wash trailers, or rake the arena." Barry's face was bright with excitement.

"Well, you sound like a man of many talents. You're certainly persuasive." Manny's eyes flicked to Cat. "With your cute little daughter, I'm sure the two of you would make a great team as barkers."

Barry laughed and put his arm around Cat. "She's more like my sister than my real sister."

His words were lost in the clatter of the trailer door opening to reveal a tall woman wrapped in a colorful swath of dark red and orange fabric. As she stepped into the trailer, her startled black eyes widened as they landed on the newcomers.

Cat noticed the overhead light casting tiny shadows from the pattern of raised dots etched over the woman's dark face, scars that intermingled with a web of age lines radiating out from beside her eyes. "Oh!" she cried, pulling back so sharply that her stethoscope swayed across her chest.

"Are you alright?" Barry asked, putting out his hand.

"Yes. Sorry I interrupted."

Barry raised his hand as if he wanted to touch her face. "Does it hurt?"

The woman slid her finger down a row of her scars. "It doesn't hurt anymore than the mark on your neck hurts you."

Barry touched his birthmark. "It doesn't hurt at all. I was born with it. Were you born with yours?"

"No. Mine were made when I was a child. My auntie said they would make me beautiful."

"You are beautiful," Barry said with a smile. He stuck out his fist. "Hello. I'm Barry Davies."

The woman smiled, showing large white teeth, and gripped Barry's fist in her hand. "Nice to meet you, Barry. I am Doctor Tanice Tabana." Her eyes shifted toward Cat.

"Catriona Cottle," Cat said, glancing at Barry, then back to Doctor Tabana. "Are you a real doctor?"

"Yes. I am the doctor for the Curious Circus."

"Then would you please look at Barry's head? He got hurt yesterday."

Barry touched his wound as if surprised to find it still there.

"Of course. Will you come to my trailer, Barry?"

Manny stood. "I didn't realize you were injured, young man."

"I feel wonderful, sir. I'm not hurt too much to be the best Barker you ever had. Me and Cat."

"No doubt. I'm willing to give you a try. Would you be willing to work a couple of weeks for room and board, just to see how it goes, before signing on permanently?"

Barry was nodding before Manny finished speaking.

"That's fine, then. Let Tanice check you out, then go on over to the costume trailer to get measured for jackets and hats."

Barry grinned. "We get to wear uniforms?"

"Certainly. Go ahead and take trailer 4. It was vacated at the last town by Leonard the Leopard Man, who fell in love with, would you believe it? A woman who raises rabbits." Manny chuckled.

Barry pointed to his birthmark. "Maybe I could be your new leopard man."

Manny nodded, smiling. "Maybe if you color in a few more spots, but for now, I need you to sell tickets. So, do we have a deal?" He put out his hand. Barry took it and gave it a firm shake.

Manny turned to Cat, hand extended. Cat looked at it, then up at the laugh lines radiating from the ringmaster's eyes. She accepted his hand again, which was large enough to fold around hers. She basked in the rush of acceptance from this man, for her and for anyone else who didn't belong anywhere else. Cat relaxed for the first time in days. They were safe.

Chapter 16

Sergeant Walters sat at his desk chair and dialed the Davies' home phone number again, counting the rings until Marlow's bright voice came on the recording just as it had before. "Thank you for calling the Davies residence. Please leave a message and we'll get back to you as soon as we can."

Charlie cleared his throat. "Hello, Mrs. Davies, this is Sergeant Walters in Salisbury again. As I said before, I'm, uh, just making a routine check on Catriona Cottle. I'd like to know how she's doing, and, well, also to know how you're faring with her under your roof. Please call back at any time, day or night. Have a nice day, ma'am."

A dark feeling slid through him as he hung up and searched his database again, which still revealed no other contact number for Marlow Reid Davies. Cat's last message said she needed a lion. He certainly wasn't living up to her expectations. What was going on over there across the Atlantic? Why wasn't this woman answering his calls? He pounded the desk in frustration.

"Hello?"

Charlie turned to see Ellie Chu standing in the doorway in a white jacket, black hair spilling over her shoulders, dark eyes watching him intently as she gripped Quigley's leash. "Is this a good time?"

Charlie broke into a smile as Quigley surged forward. "It's a perfect time." Charlie rubbed Quigley's head.

"Do you remember that we're going to visit John?"

Charlie looked up into Ellie's gentle eyes. "I didn't know it was that time yet."

"It's a little early, but I thought we might pick up a gift for him along the way."

"Certainly." Charlie stood and took the leash, putting his free arm around Ellie's waist. "What are we going to get for the old man?"

Ellie gave a little laugh. "I'm telling him you said that."

"Good. Then he'll get roused enough to make a comeback, and it'll be just like in the office again."

Leaving the station, they walked from shop to shop, considering and discarding several possible gifts until they finally browsed a charity shop. That's where Charlie found a paperweight sculpted into a tawny lion, his full mane nearly obscuring a little white lamb lying at his side. "This is it," Charlie said, picking it up.

"It's nice enough," Ellie said, taking the paperweight and turning it over, "but why this?"

Charlie told her about John's mother's "Lyon" maiden name while they headed for the checkout. Once they settled in the car with Quigley's head hanging over the back seat between them, he added, "Cat's last email said that she could use a lion right now, so this morning I finally told her who I was. I didn't mean for her to think she's been emailing John all this time. I've just been so busy that I simply replied to her emails from John's account and forgot to sign my name. I've been so worried about her that I've called the Davies' house several times, but no one's answered."

"Being in a new place is bound to require some adjustment," Ellie said. "You don't think she's in any real danger, do you?"

"All I know for sure is that I don't have a good feeling

about it," Charlie said. "Quigley doesn't either."

"Well, animals have a way of knowing." When Ellie stroked Quigley's neck, he stretched his nose up toward the headliner so that she could reach more of him.

At the hospital, they left Quigley in the car parked in the shade beneath a tree with the windows rolled down a few inches for air.

When they entered John's room, he gave them a thin smile. "How are you feeling?" Charlie asked, pulling a chair up to John's bedside.

John rubbed his chest. "Heartsore."

Ellie gently set the paperweight down on the little tray table at John's bedside. "We hope this helps you feel better."

John blinked at the paperweight before picking it up in his fingers and turning it over. "Why, thank you. It's just what I told Cat." His gaze drifted from the lion and lamb figure to Charlie. "Have you heard from her?"

"Sure have. She's getting on better with her cousin, Tamsin, and she's always liked being around the boy, Barrett."

"So she's getting things sorted, then?"

"Still fighting with the time zone change, but that will come. What about you? What does the doc say?"

"I'm to be released by week's end, then I'll move up to Carlisle to live with my daughter, Dasia."

Charlie whistled. "Clear up there?"

John nodded glumly. "Yeah. I'd better pack my macintosh."

"And when would you be coming back?"

John fidgeted with his bed cover. "See, that's the thing.

I'm not right sure." His voice dropped. "Maybe never."

"Well, then, we could take a road trip, couldn't we Charlie?" Ellie said, laying a hand on John's shoulder. "We can't be letting him get away that easy."

"We'll bring the dog," Charlie said. "He'll get you outside for some exercise. That'll keep you young."

At the end of their visit, John took hold of Charlie's outstretched hand while cradling the lion and lamb figure in his other hand. "Thanks for coming. You've done me good. Please keep a look out for Cat for me, would you?"

Charlie nodded while Ellie gave John a kiss on the cheek.

They found Quigley with his nose to the window opening. He gave an impatient "woof!" as soon as he caught sight of them. Once they got in and buckled up, Charlie pulled onto the road, driving away from the police station.

Ellie watched out the window, then said, "You're going to be doing something about Catriona, aren't you?"

"I have to, El. John asked me to look out for her, and I didn't even tell him everything that's going on. I didn't want to upset him."

"Why not call the United States authorities to check on her?"

"I've thought of that. But I get the feeling Marlow can make anything look the way she wants it to. Even if things aren't right, she'll make them look right. The only way to really know how Cat is doing is to get it from her own mouth. I need to know that she's okay."

When they reached the veterinary clinic, he steered into the parking lot and turned off the car. "Come on, boy,"

Charlie said, taking Quigley's leash. "Let's get your travel vaccinations."

Chapter 17

"Marlow?" No answer. It was so quiet that Archie
thought perhaps no one was home. But that didn't make
sense. Where would she take Tamsin? The doctor always
came to the house. "Hello? Anybody here?"

Suddenly Marlow ran down the hall toward him, hands
out, palms up. "She's abandoned our daughter and
kidnapped our son!"

Archie was so startled he dropped his suitcase in the
entryway. "What?"

"My stupid sister's crazy girl took Barrett away. She
stole him!"

"How could she?" Archie asked, moving closer to
Marlow, his luggage forgotten. "He's twice her size."

"You know how," Marlow cried, her voice rising.
"He's easily swayed. She had to have told him something
to make him go with her. Maybe she said they were going
to find you, maybe she promised him candy."

"I think Barrett is smarter than that."

"How would you know? You're not around enough to
understand your own son."

When Archie took hold of his wife's shoulders, she
suddenly slumped as if glad to have someone else hold up
her weight. "When did this happen?" Archie demanded.

"Yesterday…the day before… I don't know. I haven't
slept for worrying."

"Why didn't you call me as soon as you knew they
were missing?" He gave her a little shake as if she needed
waking up. "Why didn't you tell me?"

Marlow's gaze dropped. "You have work to do."

Archie's hands tightened. "You've called the police?"

"I... I talked to someone in law enforcement."

"Who?"

"Her gaze slid up to the ceiling. Um...Sergeant Charlie Walters."

"What is he doing about it?"

She shrugged. "Police stuff."

Archie let go, and she leaned against the wall as if her legs couldn't hold her up by themselves. "What's his number?" Archie pulled out his mobile phone.

Marlow looked up at him, her eyes narrowing. "I don't know. How should I know? He called me."

Archie glanced at the wall phone's light blinking with an unheard message. As he stepped toward it, Marlow grabbed hold of his coat. "Don't bother with that. You're a busy man. Go ahead and get your suitcase, put your things away, relax, and let me take care of the household things."

This was not the Marlow Archie knew. His Marlow would complain about his suitcase in the entryway, no matter what the circumstance, and warn him to never drop it there again. Something was wrong.

He tried to pull away, but Marlow wouldn't let go. Archie ended up dragging her along behind him, his coat straining against his body as he power walked to the wall phone. "I never could understand why you wanted to keep this archaic thing," he said as he stretched out his hand and pushed the "play" button.

While Sergeant Walters' voice asked for Marlow to call him back, Marlow cried, "It's a conspiracy!"

"Your policeman is from England?" Archie asked, his astonished gaze turning back to Marlow.

"That's where she's from," Marlow answered, her voice high. "Shouldn't they handle their own messes?" Marlow suddenly let go of Archie and covered her face with her hands. "Oh, what will become of her now?"

"We'll find her," Archie assured her. "We'll find both of them."

"I mean Tamsin!" Marlow said, lifting her head, her eyes blazing. "If we don't get that girl back, what will happen to Tamsin?"

Archie stared at his wife as if seeing a stranger standing in his house. "Why are you talking about Tamsin right now when Cat and Barrett are the ones missing? Are you insane?"

Marlow's eyes turned to angry slits as she sidled over to the counter and touched the handle of one of the knives sticking out of a butcher block. "You should never say that again," she warned. "You shouldn't accuse me of being crazy when I'm just trying to protect our children." She gave him a sideways glance. "If you were any kind of father, you'd protect them, too."

"Marlow, can't you see that this situation is too big for us? I'm calling the police, the local ones."

"You can't!" Marlow cried, turning toward Archie. "They'll take her away!"

Archie stiffened at the sight of the knife clutched in Marlow's hand. "They can't take our daughter away," he said with exaggerated calm.

"They'll take Catriona," Marlow said through her teeth, as if talking to a dense child. "Then she won't cure Tamsin."

Archie's voice softened. "Oh, Marlow." He pocketed

his phone. "Come here." Ignoring the knife she held at her side, Archie held out his arms and moved toward his wife.

"No!" Marlow backed away. "Don't touch me."

"I just want to hold you." Archie lowered his arms. "I'm trying to help you."

"Then find that girl so she can heal my daughter."

"Our daughter," Archie said as Marlow spun on her heel and hurried away.

Chapter 18

Cat relaxed her mouth, the muscles at the corners throbbing from overuse. Glancing at Barry's cheerful face, she wondered how he could smile for so long. He looked genuinely happy to see a lady walking toward the ticket booth with a young boy holding her hands on either side. A man followed them, pressing a mobile phone to his ear as Barry called, "Welcome to the Curious Circus," in a voice just as excited and cheerful as when they'd first started their ticket booth shift two hours earlier.

"We bought our tickets online," the woman said.

Barry scrolled through the computer screen, then said, "Thank you, Mr. and Mrs. Paul. You and your boys will remember this fun time together for the rest of your lives."

The boys' faces lit up, their interested gazes turning toward the circus tent opening, which didn't quite let them see into the interior. As if that was her cue, Felicianna stepped out of the tent into the sunlight, her silky wrap dress open just enough at the top to reveal a glittering sequined leotard that sent sparkles out in all directions, making her appear magical. She gave the family a wave with one hand and pulled her wrap closed with the other. "Welcome to the circus," she said before moving away.

Barry tipped his hat, making the big feather in front sway. The lady smiled, and Barry said, "Enjoy the show." The father put his phone away and the family walked into the cool interior of the large tent, the boys' heads swiveling from side to side as they did their best to take everything in.

Another woman approached the ticket booth, digging through her pocketbook while five children following along behind her like ducklings. "Did you find them yet?" the tallest girl asked, flipping her long hair back over one shoulder.

"No."

Three boys descending in height, like stair steps going down from the tall girl, pushed each other around.

The woman's head snapped up. "Settle down boys!" Then she peered into her bag. "They've got to be here."

"What are we going to do?" The girl glanced at the circus tent, then back toward the parking lot behind them, then at the youngest child, a girl who seemed too old to have her thumb in her mouth.

"Welcome to the Curious Circus," Barry said. "May I help you?"

The woman looked at him through anxious eyes. "You can't do anything for me."

Barry tipped his head. "Lost keys?"

Startled, the woman nodded. The tall girl bit her lip.

"We won't know if I can help unless I try." Barry stepped out from the ticket booth and turned toward Cat. "Take care of things until I get back, okay?"

Cat's eyes widened in astonishment. She didn't know what to say to people. For most of her life, the general population avoided her as much as she did them. She didn't know much about computers, either, not as much as Barry, and she wasn't as big as him. What if someone tried barging in the tent without a ticket? How could she stop them?

"I don't know what to do," she said, her eyes pleading with Barry not to leave her alone.

Barry leaned on the counter, looked Cat in the eye, and

replied, "You know exactly what to do." Then he reached out and gave both of her shoulders a comforting squeeze with his big hands.

The warmth of his touch spread through her, infusing her with confidence. Calmed by his touch, Cat said, "Yes, I…I do." Barry pulled back and Cat studied her cousin for a moment, trying to sense if there would be any trouble if he left, but nothing came to mind.

"Lucy, take the children into the tent and find a seat," the mother said, handing their tickets to Cat.

"Everyone hold hands," Lucy commanded. "We'll make a circus train." The children obediently linked up, fumbling a bit before locking fingers together. Then Lucy led them inside.

When Cat looked up from putting their tickets into the ticket box, she saw Barry's hand resting on the mother's shoulder as they walked away.

Twenty-eight more ticket holders went into the circus tent before Barry returned with the same woman, her face transformed by a radiant smile. "Thank you again," she said as Barry resumed his position at the ticket booth. She tipped her head. "It's funny. As soon as we headed for the parking lot, I was certain we'd find them."

"It's what I do," Barry said, and gave the woman his heartbreakingly handsome smile.

The woman dug around in her purse until Cat wondered what else she'd lost. When the woman pulled out a crumpled ten dollar bill and held it toward Barry, he put his hands up. "No, thank you, ma'am, I don't need money to be happy. Use it to buy your children some popcorn."

"I'm so glad there are people like you in the world," the

mother said, dropping the money back into her purse.

"People like you, too." Barry tipped his hat, and then the smiling woman disappeared into the tent.

When the circus music began, Barry kept looking toward the entrance. It wasn't hard for Cat to sense his waves of longing. "Go ahead," she said. "You go watch the circus from the doorway and I'll take care of the stragglers. Stay close by. I'll shout if I need you."

Barry trotted over to the tent opening and looked inside.

Some latecomers pulled Cat's attention away. When she turned to check on Barry, he was nowhere in sight. Where had he gone? She had a sudden, compelling urge to go look for him, but they were assigned to man the booth for 30 minutes past opening time before the relief ticket takers showed up.

Cat tried seeing inside the tent from the booth, but couldn't see Barry. Had he gone off with some guys like the ones who'd hurt him? Forcing herself to take slow, even breaths and tune into her feelings, Cat sifted through them for any clues of trouble, but all that fluttered through her mind was joyful excitement.

Cat glanced down the midway toward the parking lot. No one was headed her way, so she dashed to the tent opening where she caught sight of Barry boosting Felicianna up onto her horse. Cat hardly recognized Abby with all the feathers and sparkling harness she wore. Felicianna herself looked like some kind of magical being with a diaphanous cape swirling behind her sparkling costume, so long it covered Abby's hindquarters. Leaning down, she hugged Barry, who stood on his toes to embrace her. Then Barry watched Felicianna ride out into the ring on her dazzling horse. He turned, caught sight of Cat, grinned, and hurried toward her. "She needed help with the horse's straps."

"Really? I'd think she's done it enough times herself."

"They're new," Barry explained. "They're kind of stiff, and my hands are stronger than hers." Then he bent and hugged Cat. "I love it here."

Chapter 19

Sergeant Charlie Walters dialed the Davies' home again. Listening to the line ring over and over, he decided it was time to leave his last message before dialing the phone number of the Morrison, New Jersey police station.

"Hello?"

The sudden sound of a male voice startled Charlie, making him wonder if he'd accidentally dialed the wrong number. "Hello?"

"Who is this?"

"Sergeant Walters from the Salisbury, England police department. Is this the Davies' residence?"

"Yes. I'm Archie Davies."

"Mr. Davies, I'm making a routine call to check on Catriona Cottle, who recently joined your household."

There was silence on the other end.

"Hello? Mr. Davies?"

"I don't know how to tell you this…"

There was another pause before Charlie asked, "Sir? What do you have to tell me?"

Archie cleared his throat. "It appears that Catriona has run away."

Charlie gasped. Of all the things he'd imagined, Cat running away was not one of them. What did she know of America? How would she get along in that strange country? All the things he'd told Cat about moving to New Jersey were wrong. He'd assured her that the change was for the best, that everything would work out with her new family. Why hadn't he listened when she'd said she didn't want to go?

Feeling sick to his stomach, he asked, "Are you sure she's not just out to market?"

"She and our son went missing last night or the night before."

"Your son is missing, too? And you don't know when?"

"I was gone on a business trip." Archie paused and his voice dropped in pitch. "My wife didn't let me know until I got home just now. She didn't want me to tell anyone."

Not tell anyone? What kind of nonsense was that? What if Cat hadn't run away at all, but had been taken against her will? As small as she was, it wouldn't be that hard to carry her off. "Have you considered that... they may have been taken by force?"

"Their packs are gone. I don't think a kidnapper would have given them time to pack their things."

"Not likely." Charlie couldn't stop the thought, *Not unless Archie's son was the abductor.* "Have you called the police?" Charlie asked.

"No. Your call came through just as I was looking up the number to make the call. Look, sir, please don't get Marlow in trouble." Archie's voice wavered. "She's not a bad person. She has just…changed since our daughter got sick. She's not the same woman I married."

"Call the police right now," Charlie commanded. "I'll be arriving on the next flight to America."

"I have another business trip..."

"It would be in your best interest to be there when I arrive," Charlie said. "I should be there in 12 hours."

Chapter 20

Thirty minutes after the circus began, Cat and Barry stood inside the tent, mesmerized by the performance, laughing at the antics, gasping at the daring of the performers, and awed by the beauty of the costumes and performers. Barry clapped loudly for Gunther as he lifted a refrigerator over his head, and Bendo the clown popped out the top. Gunther glanced over at Barry and scowled.

When it was over, Cat and Barry walked back to their assigned trailer, talking about the acrobats, Eeny, Meeny, and Miney, Feliciana, Gunther, Bendo, the animal acts, and motorbikes that seemed to defy gravity.

Once they were inside the trailer house, Cat insisted that Barry put his borrowed sleeping bag on the bed in the small bedroom. It was larger than the bed made from lowering the dining table and rearranging couch cushions on top. Even though the dining room bed was unfamiliar to her, it felt more welcoming than the neatly made guest bed in Tamsin's room.

Cat dreamed about Quigley, so happy to see her that he lept about the trailer so convincingly that she could almost believe he was actually there. When she got up to let him outside, the sky was pink with dawn. Barry ran toward them from the mess tent, then knelt and rubbed Quigley's ears as if he'd known him all his life. Quigley stretched his nose up to give Barry's birthmark a curious sniff.

Barry laughed. "Come on, boy, let's play catch!" Cat sat on the trailer steps, watching Barry throw a ball for Quigley, when a big shadow with outstretched wings like a predatory bird swooped across the ground. Startled, Cat glanced up, Barry paused in mid-throw, and Quigley jumped for the ball with an excited whine. Searching the sky, Cat saw nothing other than an expanse of blue. When a sudden whoosh of air ruffled her curls, Cat felt no fear. Instead, the passing breeze filled her with a sense of adventure that made her hug her arms across her body with happiness.

When she awoke, Cat lay still, savoring the excitement that carried over from her dream. The only thing that dampened her enthusiasm was the realization that Quigley wasn't really with her.

When Cat heard Barry stirring in his room, she sat up and called, "Didn't Doctor Tabana want to check your head again today?"

"Absolutely," Barry replied so cheerfully that it was hard to believe he had just woken up.

When they reached the medical trailer, Doctor Tabana offered Barry a chair before checking his head. The free-flowing sleeves of her purple and gold caftan nearly hid his face as she lifted her hands to part his hair. Then her eyes went wide. "I've never seen anyone heal this quickly," she said, her ritual forehead scars lifting above her raised brows.

"It doesn't need any more checking," Barry announced.

"You're right." The doctor lowered her hands. "Can you tell me why you heal faster than most people?"

"Absolutely," Barry said. "It's because I give real hugs."

Doctor Tabana offered him a patient smile. "Have you always been a fast healer?"

Barry nodded. "And if you need me to hug anyone for

you, I'll be happy to help you out." Barry stood and opened his arms. "Would you like a hug?"

Surprised, Doctor Tabana glanced at Cat. "It would not be professional," she said, "but I am happy for you and your good health."

"Thank you," Barry said, pushing his fist toward the doctor. "I am happy for you, too."

Tabana gave him a fist bump.

Once they left the medical trailer, Barry said, Let's go to the Big Top."

"There's no performance now," Cat reminded him.

"Yeah, but we can see if any animals are there."

"Alright," Cat said.

When they walked into the shade of the Big Top, the dust tickled Cat's nose, making her sneeze. When she opened her eyes, she noticed Eeny, Meeny, and Miney practicing in the ring. A feeling of dark foreboding crawled into her stomach. "Oh, no," she said.

"What's wrong?" Barry asked, his arm sliding around Cat in a comforting circle of warmth.

"Nothing's wrong with me. It's Miney."

Barry glanced at the muscular acrobat balancing Meeny on his knee before giving him a mighty flip. Meeny spun in a circle and landed on his feet. "That's terrific!" Barry cried, clapping in appreciation.

"He's hurting," Cat murmured, drawing up her leg a little as a burning feeling radiated from her knee and another burning sensation slid down from her shoulder.

"What's hurting him?"

"Something in his knee, and in his shoulder." Cat stared at Miney, trying to pinpoint his problem. "It's... I don't know. Old wounds or arthritis or pulled muscles or something."

She turned toward Barry, but he wasn't there anymore. He was striding toward Miney, his long arms outstretched.

"Barry!" she called, hurrying after him, but before she could reach him, he bent down and grabbed Miney with both arms.

Miney flinched and pushed at Barry. "Get off me!"

Barry stumbled back.

"You're just weird, man."

Barry stuck his hands out to his sides. "Why?"

Miney's gaze was serious. "Guys don't hug guys."

"I hug my dad."

"You're related."

"So are we."

"What?" Miney's voice rose in disbelief. "How?"

"We're both part of the circus family."

Eeny and Meeny laughed while Miney relaxed. "I see. Well, if it will make you go away and leave us alone to practice, then I'll hug you, but only if they will, too." He thrust his thumb toward his companions.

"Absolutely!" Barry bent and opened his arms wide. "I can hug all three of you at once."

The three men looked at one another.

"Is he for real?" Eeny asked.

"He's like no one I've ever known," Meeny replied.

"I think we should just play along and get it over with," Miney said.

"Barry, you shouldn't..." Cat began, but Miney cut her off.

"He's just a big kid," he said. "Come on, guys, let's

man up."

The three acrobats moved closer to Barry, but Eeny stopped just out of Barry's reach.

"This is crazy," Meeny said, launching himself into a somersault that landed him on Barry's back. He hung on while Barry wobbled, startled by the sudden shift in gravity. Eeny and Miney rushed into grab Barry's arms, and he hung onto them for support. When he found his balance, he said, "Thanks, guys." Breathing hard, he said, "I thought I was going to fall."

"You okay now?" Eeny asked, pulling back and looking into Barry's face.

Miney stayed where he was a few seconds longer, his face turned in against Barry's chest, eyes closed.

Keeping an arm tight around Miney, Barry said, "Almost," and took in another deep breath.

Meeny slid off Barry's back. "Sorry for rockin' the boat. I've a touch of claustrophobia, and couldn't see myself squished up against those two. Not sure they remembered their deodorant this morning."

Miney sighed and pushed away from Barry, who let him loose and stood up straight. "Thanks, guys. Now I'm off to see the elephants."

"If you get in hugging range of their trunks, they may be happy to play your silly game," Meeny said with a laugh.

Barry grinned. "I hadn't thought of that."

"So, stop thinking about it already," Miney said. "He's just kidding. You can't trust those elephants."

"At least not until I make friends with them," Barry said, striding towards the exit while Eeny, Meeny, and

Miney got back to work on their routine.

Before Cat could follow, Bendo walked up beside her. Startled, she glanced up to see his gaze burning into Barry's back. "Is something wrong?" she asked.

"It looked like there was trouble."

"None here."

"Surely he causes you trouble," Bendo insisted.

"If anything, Barry gets me out of trouble."

Bendo folded his arms and looked down at Cat with a half smile curving his narrow lip. "I assure you, you don't have to cover for him, not with me." His voice dropped to a conspiratorial tone. "You see, unlike most people, I know what it's like." When Cat didn't answer, Bendo leaned closer. "Don't believe me? It's a fact. I have a brother like him. My parents called him 'Special,' but I called him 'Spaz'."

Cat's eyes narrowed as a wave of apprehension washed over her. "Why would you call him that?"

"Why not?" Bendo picked at some invisible thing on his sleeve. "He called me 'Toothpick,' while he ate everything in sight." Bendo snorted. "Our parents got him anything he wanted; ice cream, candy, a new bike, even though he could barely ride it and ended up smashing it."

"Barry's not like that."

Bendo relaxed, his voice warming with the sense of a shared confidence. "That's what they keep telling you, but you've got to look at it for yourself." He patted Cat's arm with jerky movements that felt as if she were being pecked at by a predatory bird. "I just want you to know that I truly understand what it's like to live with someone like that. I understand so well, because my brother was the older one, too. When he learned that he could blame me for the trouble he caused, he made getting me in trouble his hobby." Bendo straightened and stared off across the arena. "He knew exactly what he was doing, looking directly at me before spilling, dropping, cutting, or stealing. Then he'd act dumber than he was, blame me, and I'd get in trouble."

Cat meant it when she said, "I'm so sorry."

Bendo put his slim hand on Cat's shoulder. She didn't dare move out from under it. Something about this man felt fragile as glass, and if broken, the sharp edges would cut someone. His voice softening to a conspiratorial whisper, Bendo said. "I assure you, I'm your friend. You can tell me anything."

"Thank you," Cat said through a throat so tight that her words felt strangled. She reached into her pocket, but her colorful hat wasn't there. She'd left it in the trailer. "I need to go now."

"Of course." Bendo slid his hand off of her shoulder, and Cat escaped.

Moving down the midway in search of Barry, Cat noticed the man with the squashed face setting up a game called, "Mouse Catch." It sounded so similar to "Mouse Trap" that she stopped, staring at the dizzying array of stuffed mice hanging from the three sides of the game tent.

"You like mice?" the man asked, his expression so warm that Cat stepped closer to him.

"Not especially, but I know someone who does."

The man nodded. "Your brother." He flung his hand out as if to encompass the world. "He seems to like everything." He smiled at Cat, which made his face look even more squashed. "My name is Mus."

"I'm Cat."

Mus chuckled. "It is the same name in my country. Now we are Cat and Mus."

"Does 'mus' mean 'mouse?'"

"Jah." He studied Cat for a moment. "While we wait to open the midway, you play my game."

Cat shook her head. "I have no money."

Mus swept his hand around his booth as if clearing all the mice off the walls. "Not this game." He pulled out a plastic bowl, cardboard 12 inches square with a faded yellow wheel of cheese painted on it, and two wooden mice with strings for tails. "This game."

"What's it called?"

"Whatever you wish," Mus said. "Come. I have an extra chair."

Cat glanced down the midway. Should she keep looking for Barry? He wasn't anywhere in sight. Closing her eyes, she took a deep breath. She could wait to find him.

Curious about the game, she went inside the booth and sat opposite Mus.

"This can be with more players, but two is enough, because all we need is a cat and a mouse," Mus explained. "Since you have the name, you start at being the cat. Here. You hold the yogurt container that is now a mouse trap. Roll the die." Mus tossed a large die with colorful dots onto the cardboard. It stopped with six red dots facing up. "Ah! Mus cried. "That is the signal! A six or a one means you drop the trap down on the mice. When I see six or a one, I pull on their tails, like so." He gave both wooden mouse tails a tug, one with each hand, sliding them off the board.

"If you catch them, then you get a point for each. If you don't, then I get a point for each one that escaped. See? When one of us reaches ten points, then we change places." Cat rolled the die. Before long, she was slapping down her yogurt container and laughing along with Mus as the scores piled up. Mus won the first game, then it was Cat's turn to hold the mice by their tails and watch the numbers on the die. After they'd played several rounds, Mus said, "You are getting better."

"Barry would love this game," Cat said. "He has a game called 'Mouse Trap,' but it's more complicated. I understand this one much better."

"Then it is yours."

"Oh, no," Cat said, jumping to her feet. "I can't take your game."

"I tell you what." Mus stood, facing Cat nearly eye to eye. "I will go to lunch and eat another container of yogurt. I will get another piece of cardboard from the cooks. Painting a another cheese will give me something new to do, and I will give a new pair of mice a chance to play." He pulled a box out from under the table, lifted the lid, and turned it so Cat saw that it was full of wooden string-tailed mice. "They are consolation prizes I made. I do not like to see children go away empty handed if they do not win a big stuffed mouse."

Cat gave him a hesitant smile. "If you're sure."

"I am certain. Here, two more mice for if you have more friends to play." Mus put two more mice in the yogurt container and handed it to Cat. "Now it is lunchtime. You go teach your brother how to play, and don't let him cheat!"

"He would never do that," Cat assured him. "Thank you, Mus!"

Cat headed for the mess tent, but didn't see Barry inside. She was so hungry that she filled a plate and sat facing the entrance to watch for him. She had taken the her bite and the lunch crowd was dwindling when Barry finally strode into the mess tent, leading a little gray short-haired dog wearing something colorful on its head. When Cat looked closer, she saw that it was a little flowered bathing cap buckled beneath the animal's gray chin.

The dog wasn't the only one with Barry. On one side of him walked a woman with so many pins in her face that she hardly looked human. On his other side was a man with a large hump on his back. Barry looped the dog's leash around his arm to get his food while his companions filled plates and chatted with him like a new best friend.

As soon as Barry saw Cat, he smiled and headed her way, sitting next to her while the others took seats across from them.

"This is Penny Pierce," Barry said, pointing to the lady with the piercings. The metal rods and rings in Penny's cheeks and lips pushed up as she smiled and waggled a greeting with fingers covered in so many rings that they looked as if they belonged on a robot. "She does a magnet act, creating sculptures on her face like the Eiffel Tower, Statue of Liberty, and Mt. Rushmore."

Cat raised her eyebrows.

"Don't worry, I don't do it while eating, honey," Penny said around a tongue heavily pierced with dainty metal rods.

"And Denny Hill is the best horse and dog trainer this

side of Calcutta," Barry announced.

"If I do say so myself," Denny said, looking up from his plate with a forehead so creased with lines that it looked as if his skin had been folded like a paper fan. He gave Cat an infectious grin.

"Hello," Cat said, returning the smile.

"Denny trained Seal Dog, here." Barry looked down at the dog sitting beside the bench, looking up at him with a hopeful gaze. "She's performing for the first time tonight, so she gets a special lunch. Right, girl?"

Seal Dog wagged her tail and cocked her flowered swim cap to one side.

"Pardon me," Denny said to Cat, "but it's kind of funny, you being called 'Cat.' I'd peg you for more of a dog person."

"I have a dog," Cat said to Denny, impressed by his insight. "His name is Quigley, but he lives in the U.K."

"That's a ways to go walk him."

"Well, he can't live with me just now." Cat lowered her head. "I miss him."

Denny reached out and patted her hand. "I can see you do. I hope you get back together real soon."

Tears welled up in Cat's eyes. Before they fell, Barry jumped up and handed Seal Dog's leash to her. "There's Gunther! I'm going to ask him to sit with us."

As he bounded off, Penny lowered her eyelids, each weighed down with a little dumbbell, a glittering stud, and a gold ring. "He won't."

Cat watched the big man turn in the lunch line when Barry hurried up to him and gestured toward their table. "Why not?"

Penny shrugged. "He never eats with anyone. He comes at the end of the meal and takes his food out to his trailer to eat by himself."

As Cat watched, Gunther shook his head and backed away from Barry. Barry turned and headed back toward their table.

"What did he say?" Cat asked as Barry sat down and took Seal Dog's leash.

Barry was unusually somber when he said, "He doesn't want to sit by people. I don't understand. He wouldn't explain."

"Don't feel bad," Denny said. "He's always like that."

"Maybe someone hurt him when he was little," Barry said. Raising his eyes, he watched Gunther in the food line, hesitating behind someone who'd gone back for seconds. "He's got all those scars on his head."

"It's hard to imagine anyone being able to hurt that mountain of a man," Penny said.

"There are other ways to get hurt besides your body," Barry explained, touching his chest. "Your soul can hurt where no one can see."

Chapter 21

Archie closed his suitcase, clicked the lock shut, carried it to the front door, and took hold of the doorknob. But instead of twisting it open, he stood still for a long moment, feeling curiously conflicted. He'd never been plagued with indecision before. He should go. He was expected at the meeting. It wouldn't be right to make excuses, but something held him back. It wasn't that policeman from the U.K. He had no jurisdiction over Archie, who was an American citizen under U.S. law. Archie wasn't Barrett's only parent, either, nor the official guardian for Catriona. The welfare for both of them could legally fall to Marlow.

What could Archie do about either of them anyway? He didn't know where they were. He'd done his duty by calling the authorities. But for the first time in a long time, Archie felt a tug to stay home.

Dropping his hand from the knob, he set his luggage on the floor. Frustrated, he strode into the living room where he sat on the couch until the restlessness built up to the point that he pushed himself to his feet and paced back and forth. At last, seemingly on their own, his feet carried him down the hallway to Tamsin's room. He discovered that the door was slightly open. Everything inside was quiet. Archie tapped lightly, hoping not to wake his daughter if she was sleeping.

"Who is it?" Tamsin's voice sounded faint.

"It's me. Your father."

A moment of silence. Then she said, "Come in."

Archie pushed the door open to see Tamsin lying on her pillow, skin so pale she looked like a beautiful ghost. He made himself smile. "How are you feeling?"

"Tired."

Archie paused. "Do you want to sleep?"

"No, Daddy, I'm tired of sleeping."

Archie stepped inside, pushed the door closed, and sat on the chair by Tamsin's bed. "Do you know one of my favorite reasons I'm glad you're my daughter?"

"What?"

"The hairstyling parties."

At Tamsin's look of confusion, Archie explained, "When you were little, there were times I'd be reading the paper and you'd come up behind me with a comb. You'd comb my hair and spray it with hairspray and comb it some more. When you were done, you'd carry your brush and comb around to my lap and ask me to make your hair into a ponytail or braid."

"I remember!" Tamsin said, breaking into a thin smile.

"I wasn't very good at it, I'm afraid. But you were."

"Oh, you aren't as bad as Cat, believe me."

"She doesn't know how to style hair?"

"Not a bit." Tamsin looked up at the ceiling, her eyes filling with tears.

"What's wrong, honey?"

Tamsin shrugged.

"What can I do?"

"Nothing."

"Please tell me what's the matter." He took his daughter's hand.

"It's just that I'm afraid I wasn't very nice to her."

"You're a nice person, honey."

A tear escaped Tamsin's eye and rolled down the side

of her face. "Maybe I used to be."

Archie leaned over and carefully wrapped his arms around his daughter's shoulders. "You still are. I love you so much. You're the best daughter I could ever wish for, beautiful inside and out."

"Oh, Daddy." Tamsin's voice was choked with tears. "I don't deserve you."

"You deserve better than me," Archie whispered. He bit his lip, trying to keep his voice steady. "I haven't let you know how much you mean to me lately. I'm going to be a better father to you from now on."

"Thank you." Tamsin sniffed. "I would hug you back, Dad, but you're holding my arms down."

With choked laughter, Archie let up the pressure so that Tamsin could push her thin arms around his neck. Her pressure was so slight that Archie could barely feel her touch. After a moment, she relaxed and her arms slid free. He pulled back and looked down at her face, the tear tracks still glistening as they radiated from her closed eyes. She wore a smile, even in her exhaustion.

Archie stayed a moment more, studying his little girl's face. Then he tenderly pulled the blankets up to her shoulders and crept to the doorway. As he stepped into the hallway, Marlow nearly ran into him. "What are you doing?" she asked, her voice sharp.

"Visiting Tamsin."

"Why?" She tried to push past him.

Archie blocked his wife. "She just fell asleep. Let her rest."

Marlow's eyebrows rose. "Who are you to tell me how to take care of my daughter?"

"Our daughter."

"Oh, so now she's our daughter? What made you care?"

"I've always cared."

"Who feeds her, cleans her, and keeps her company while you are off on your business trips?"

"I'm just trying to make a living. You knew what my job was when you married me."

"When I married you, how many years ago? I thought you'd be company president by now so you could make your own hours. Other men who travel for work spend more time with their children than you do."

Archie rubbed his forehead. "Okay, Marlow, maybe you're right. When our little girl was diagnosed as terminal, I didn't know how to handle it. I was scared to spend time with her because I didn't know when we'd lose her."

Marlow's words punched through the air. "We're not going to lose her. Don't ever say that again." Her voice lowered into a churlish tone. "And do you know what? I'm glad you're not the company president. Things are better around here when you're gone. So why not do what you do best? Leave. Go and find Catriona before it's too late."

Stung, Archie asked, "What about Barrett?"

"You can find him if you want to, but in case you've forgotten, he'll be eighteen next month. At eighteen, he doesn't have to do anything I say. He already ran away from home, so what makes you think he even wants to come back?"

Marlow pushed against Archie's chest. "Now let me in there. You may not want to be with Tamsin, but I do, even if it's just to watch her sleep." When Archie moved aside, Marlow plunged into their daughter's room and shut the door behind her.

Archie stared at the closed door, wondering how Marlow had changed so much without him noticing. She was right about one thing. He hadn't been around enough.

Archie went back to the foyer, picked up his suitcase, and carried it into his bedroom. He wasn't going anywhere until that British police officer showed up.

Chapter 22

Reluctantly turning Seal Dog's leash over to Denny, Barry walked toward the ticket booth while Cat did her best to keep pace with him. "Do you know everyone in the Curious Circus?" she asked.

"Not yet, but I will."

"Hey," Miney said, pulling up beside them.

"Hello," Barry greeted him with a wide smile.

He shortened his step while Cat gave Miney a questioning look. "Where are your brothers?"

"Meeny's my brother," Miney explained. "Eeny's my cousin."

"I have a cousin," Barry said, "but my brother is actually a sister."

Miney stared up at him for a moment, then burst into laughter. "I like you, you know? I really like you." He swung his arm around and up over his head. "Hey, Barry, I don't know what happened this morning, but ever since, you, you know," he looked over his shoulder, then turned back and whispered, "hugged us, I don't have that pain in my joints anymore."

Barry put his fist out. "Glad I could help."

Miney made a fist and touched it to Barry's. "Yeah!" Barry said. Then his gaze slid past Miney and he grinned. "There goes Rhoda to feed the elephants! I'm going to help. See you later, alligator!"

"We don't have any alligators," Miney joked.

"Sometimes Gunther acts like an alligator," Barry said just before he trotted off.

"Oh, no," Cat murmured.

"What?"

"Gunther's in his way."

Gunther turned around before Barry reached him. Backing up, he raised his fists. Barry said something to him and Gunther shook his head with an expression that resembled fear. Barry's shoulders slumped and he moved around Gunther to catch up to Rhoda.

"What is his problem?" Cat asked, hating to see Barry so sad. "He doesn't have to be so mean."

"Gunther's not mean. He's scared."

Cat knew deep inside that Miney was right, but she couldn't figure out why. "What could he possibly be scared of?"

Miney was quiet for a moment. Then he said, "A broken heart."

"Why?"

Miney sighed. "He lost his mother, father and little brother in a boating accident. He tried to save them, even grabbed onto some flesh he felt underwater, but before he could surface, the propeller cut his head, knocking him unconscious. When his little brother's body was found, he had fresh red marks on his neck from Gunther's fingers. Since then, Gunther worked out his grief in the gym. He refuses to get close to anyone because he's afraid he might lose people he loves again."

"I should have known that."

"How could you?" Miney asked. "I only know because his cousin came to visit, and he wouldn't even hug her." Miney grinned. "But she hugged me."

Cat laughed. "Lucky you." Then she fixed Miney with a serious gaze. "Thank you for putting up with Barry."

"He's cool." Miney swung his arm again. "I just don't know how he does his magic."

"It's in his hugs," Cat said. "Love works miracles."

"Yeah," Miney said with a wave as he started off toward the midway. "Whatever."

Cat arrived at the ticket booth in her crimson uniform before Barry. Glancing in all directions, she hoped to see him heading her way. At last, one minute before she was scheduled to open, a breathless Barry came running up to the booth, his hat crooked.

"Where were you?" Cat asked.

"Doing circus stuff."

Even though he'd arrived, Barry didn't stay in the booth. He kept walking to the tent door and peering inside, then coming back to the ticket booth. After his fifth trip to the tent, Cat asked, "Looking for Felicianna?"

"No. Why would I do that?"

"Because you like her."

"I like you, too, but right now I need to make sure Seal Dog's bathing cap is fastened tight. We were having trouble with the snap earlier. If it's not tight enough, she could get water in her ears."

"I don't think water hurts a dog's ears."

"Seal dog doesn't actually have any ears, not on the outside." Barry looked pained. "Whoever had her as a puppy cut them off clear to her head. Denny says if she dives into the water and it slaps into her ear canals, it could hurt her."

"Then why in the world did they train her to be a diving dog?"

"They didn't. She did it herself. After being rescued,

she jumped in the water to swim. Then she jumped in from a higher place. When Denny tried even higher jumps, Seal Dog loved it. That's how she became Seal Dog. Denny says when she first comes out into the ring, she doesn't have her cap on. Her smooth head makes her look like a real seal, but with dog legs. Then they put the cap on and she does her tricks."

"I'm sure Denny will fasten her bathing cap properly."

"I still want to cheer her on. Even though someone was mean to her, she turned it into something nice, and now her life is fun."

Cat didn't miss the wistful tone in Barry's voice. "How about the elephants?" she joked. "Don't they deserve cheering on, too?"

"Absolutely! You're the best, Cat. I knew you'd understand!" He stuck out his fist, and Cat tapped her knuckles against his.

Cat took most of the late-comer's tickets because Barry had his head inside the tent. Thirty minutes after showtime started, Cat and Barry found a seat at the edge of the bleachers. But unlike the night before, Cat felt a rising sense of restlessness.

As soon as Seal Dog trotted out, Barry clapped while Cat marveled at how much the dog's sleek head really did look like a seal's. In fact, her whole body was so seal-like that Cat could almost believe she was one, except that seals don't have four trotting legs. Seal Dog was a crowd favorite when she held still for her little flowered cap to be snapped on, then scampered up the ladder to the diving board. She splashed into the water to thunderous applause.

After the dog made her exit, Cat's sense of foreboding

grew stronger as Bendo strolled into the ring. He lived up
to his name by bending over a leather suitcase with wheels,
examining it as if he'd never seen one before. After
opening the lid and folding himself inside, a fluffy little
dog jumped on the lid and closed it. A clown in a fat, puffy
costume picked up the suitcase handle and rolled it along
behind him as he pretended to run for a train. The suitcase
was comically traded among different clown performers
before a big clown with long eyelashes opened the case and
Bendo came out. When the big clown chased him around
the ring with puckered lips, Bendo dove back into the
leather case and the dog shut him in again.

Barry laughed in delight while Cat scanned the tent,
wondering what was wrong. She didn't know. What good
were premonitions if she couldn't do anything about them?
Frustrated, she decided to go back to the trailer. If she was
curled up under a blanket, she might not feel like it was her
fault if something bad happened.

Just as she started to tell Barry she was leaving,
Felicianna rode into the ring, standing on Abby's back, her
diaphanous cape flowing along behind her under the
spotlight, transforming her into a magical butterfly girl. She
rode all the way around the ring. When she got back to her
starting point, Denny stepped forward from the shadows
and raised his hands, ready to catch the cape as Felicianna
flipped open the clasp with one hand and shrugged it off
her shoulders. But instead of floating free, the clasp caught
on Felicianna's leotard. The fabric sagged, catching in
Abby's hoof. The horse fell forward with an equine scream.

Arms out, Felicianna flew over Abby's head, the
momentum burying the clasp deeper into her costume so

that her body was pulled back by the cape still bound around her horse's hoof. She landed with a sickening thud amid a puff of delicate fabric.

Barry was up and running toward Felicianna before she even hit the ground. Manny ran across the ring and blocked him. When Barry pushed past him, Manny grabbed his arm. Barry dragged the ringmaster along until Gunther galloped across the ring and caught Barry in a bear hug.

"I need to help her!" Barry cried, stretching his hand toward the fallen girl.

"Let the medical personnel do their job," Manny answered, nodding to a knot of people surrounding Felicianna, their jackets decorated with the medical rod of Asclepius on their sleeves.

"But I can help!" Barry's gaze was glued to Felicianna.

Denny held Abby's sparkling halter as the horse kicked her hind hoof, even though the fabric was no longer wrapped around it. Denny gave Feliciana a sorrowful look from beneath his wrinkled brow, then dropped his gaze to Abby's skinned knee. Then he trudged out of the arena, pulling the horse behind him.

Doctor Tabana hurried into the tent, her blue and gold tie-dyed tunic flowing behind her as the medical personnel made a space for her to kneel at Felicianna's side.

"See, she is being taken care of," Manny assured Barry. "You can see her later."

Barry's face crumpled and he stopped straining against Gunther's grip. Manny patted Gunther's arm and the strong man relaxed his hold. With a sob, Barry turned and wrapped his arms around Gunther, crying into the big man's leopard print leotard as if he would never stop.

Gunther paused a moment before putting his arms around Barry and laying his head on top of Barry's.

Cat crept up to Barry's side and took hold of his sleeve. It was a long moment before he let go of Gunther, but as soon as he did, Cat took his hand and led him into their trailer. Barry stood by the closed door while Cat pulled out the game Mus had given her. "Play with me," she said.

Barry watched Cat lay out the cardboard and the four mice on the painted cheese wheel. Then she handed him the die and held the plastic container over the board. Barry dropped the die and Cat slapped the yogurt cup over the mice. "You're supposed to pull the mice out on a six or a one," Cat said. "You're not even trying."

"I can't." Barry ran his fingers through his hair. "I have to make Felicianna all right." Barry twisted the doorknob.

"Wait!" But Barry didn't wait. He went out the door while Cat scrambled to stand up. By the time she got to the door, Barry was nowhere in sight.

Cat scampered down the steps to go in search of him, but a voice stopped her cold.

"I wouldn't bother if I were you."

Cat gave a start as she recognized Bendo standing beside the trailer. "Oh! I didn't see you there."

"They brought in the elephants to distract the audience from Felicianna."

"I don't care about elephants. I've got to find Barry so he doesn't get into trouble."

"Why? If your brother can get you in trouble, then let him go ahead and get into some trouble of his own."

Cat's anger rose until she shouted, "You don't know anything! He's not even my brother!"

Bendo's eyes widened in surprise. "Who is he then? Surely not your…husband?"

"Don't be ridiculous. He's my cousin."

"Your cousin? Then how can he be your guardian?"

"He's not! He's only seventeen."

"Is that so?"

Cat hurried past Bendo toward the Big Top where Manny stood outside with Barry. "Is she okay?" Barry asked.

"We don't know yet. We'll know after she goes to the hospital."

"Please let me see her," Barry begged, his eyes welling with tears.

"You're a very caring person, Barry, but she needs trained medical help right now."

"I know you don't understand, but I can help her."

Manny hesitated.

"He can," Cat urged. "What will it hurt to let him try? All he wants to do is hug her."

Manny looked from Cat to Barry and back again. "I'll see what I can do."

Manny turned and ducked inside the tent. Barry followed with Cat right behind him. They followed Manny to a stretcher where Felicianna lay strapped on a hard board with a wide brace around her neck. Doctor Tabana stood beside her, her face grim. Without breaking stride, Barry headed straight for Felicianna.

An ambulance siren sounded in the distance just as Doctor Tabana moved in to block Barry. "No!" she said. "If you touch her, you may paralyze her." She cast a worried glance at the horseback rider and added, "If she's not paralyzed already."

"I can help her," Barry said.

Tabana was firm. "Once she's in the hospital and stabilized, I'll take you to see her. But you can't touch her now."

"I've got to!" Barry stared at Felicianna.

"I know you care," Doctor Tabana said, her voice softening. "I care, too. That's why I can't let you get close to her."

Cat stepped up close enough to take Doctor Tabana's hand. "He really can help."

Tabana put her other hand on Cat's curly hair. "How? He has no training."

"There are other things that can cure," Cat said, her eyes steady on the doctor's. "You know there are."

Tabana studied Cat's eyes before pulling away. "I'm sorry. This is a different world from my childhood one. There are different rules."

Cat's gaze shifted to a movement on the ladder leading up to the trapeze. It was Eeny, climbing up rung by rung. What was he doing? He wasn't part of the trapeze act.

Cat jumped when Meeny yelled, "Hey! What are you doing up there?"

Everyone's faces swiveled upward to the platform as Eeny climbed up onto it. He waved at the onlookers, then reached up toward the trapeze. "Get down!" Doctor Tabana called as she took three strides toward the ladder.

The gurney carrying Felicianna suddenly rolled toward Barry. Without hesitation, Barry stepped forward to meet it. Leaning over, he circled his arms around Felicianna's body like a big warm halo. Meeny and Miney scuttled out from beneath the gurney as Barry murmured, "You are a good, loving friend, Felicianna. You want to get well, Abby wants you to get well, we all want you to. Please take this get-well hug from your whole circus family."

The ambulance pulled up beside the tent and medical personnel hopped out, converging on Barry, pushing him aside as they surrounded Felicianna. Eeny climbed down the ladder as the circus performers who weren't in the ring watched the patient loaded into the ambulance.

A police car pulled up beside the ambulance, blue and red lights whirling as two policemen got out of the car and approached Barry. "Barrett Davies?" one of them asked.

"Absolutely," Barry said, sticking his fist out toward the officer, "but I like 'Barry' better."

The policeman's gaze flickered to Barry's fist as his hand went to the butt of his gun. "You are under arrest for kidnapping."

Chapter 23

"You are not to be trusted," Marlow snarled, pulling Catriona into the house by the arm. "I can't believe what you did, you evil girl."

"Mom?" Tamsin's voice sounded faintly down the hall. Marlow froze. "Yes, dear?"

"Is Catriona here?"

Marlow gave Cat's arm a shake and hissed, "Don't do anything stupid." In a louder, sweeter voice, she replied, "Yes, she's here."

"I want to see her."

"No," Cat whimpered.

"What did you say?" Marlow looked stricken as she stared down at her niece.

"I don't want to go in there."

"She's family," Marlow said between clenched teeth. "You will go, and you will be nice, or else." Marlow started down the hall, dragging Cat along. In a slightly breathless voice, she called out cheerily, "We're coming."

Marlow pushed Cat into the room and stood in the doorway, blocking her escape.

Cat reluctantly looked at Tamsin lying on her bed. The girl seemed all but transparent, her skin pale, her hair spread so thinly across the pillow that it looked like golden spiderwebs. Tamsin put her hand out, but she didn't lift her head from her pillow. "I missed you."

Cat stayed near the door until Marlow gave her a shove. "I'm sorry," Cat said.

"Well," Marlow said into the silence, as cheerily as if the girls had just met for a birthday party. "Can I get you anything?"

"Mashed potatoes," Tamsin said.

"Oh." Marlow's voice faltered. "Mashed?"

"Yes. Real potatoes." Tamsin took a breath. "And country gravy." Another breath. "Your homemade, Mother, so good."

Marlow's brow creased in confusion, but she said, "All right, darling. I'll be back."

After she left, Tamsin slid her hand across her covers. "Please... sit by me?"

Cat didn't want to. She wanted to get out of this room, out of this house, out of this town, and out of this country. She longed to be across the Atlantic Ocean.

Tamsin sighed. "I sent Mother..." she took a shallow breath, "...so she wouldn't hover."

"Could I..." Cat stopped and looked down at her hands.

"What?" Tamsin asked.

"Could I please use your computer?"

Tamsin paused, then answered, "Not long. I'd like... talk."

"I'll hurry," Cat promised, striding across the room to the white computer next to Tamsin's bed. She called up her email and composed a message to John Lamb.

"Please let me come home. I don't belong here. If you don't come get me, I'll have to run away again."

After she hit "send," she closed the computer window and turned around to see Tamsin watching her with tears in her eyes. The sparkling pools made Tamsin appear as insubstantial as an angel. "Are you hurting somewhere?" Cat asked.

"Not my body."

"Then what are you crying about?"

"Scared. I feel better... when you're here."

"Me?"

Tamsin nodded, her hair bunching and smoothing on her pillow with each movement.

"But why?"

"You're calm. You... know things... what's coming."

Cat put her palms out toward Tamsin. "I'm not always calm, and I don't always know what's going to happen."

Tamsin fumbled her hand across her blanket, reaching for Cat's hand. Cat reluctantly met it. Tamsin couldn't hold on tightly, but her fingers pressed against Cat's as gently as a kitten. "What's happening to me, Cat?"

Avoiding Tamsin's eyes, Cat twisted her head toward the computer, wishing that Officer Lamb could come through the screen and take her home right now.

"You know."

Cat turned back to see Tamsin's face in soft repose. She'd always been so demanding, and now she was as calm as a leaf on a still lake.

Cat sighed. "Do you really want to hear?"

Tamsin's mouth turned up in a slight smile, and her eyes widened. "You saw."

Cat hesitated, then slowly nodded.

"Tell me."

When Cat bit her lips together and shifted her gaze, Tamsin's voice softened. "Please. I won't tell... Mother."

Cat let out a breath. "Alright. You are going to one of the most beautiful places I've ever seen."

Tamsin increased the pressure on Cat's hand, although

it only felt like a bug walking across her skin.

"Tell me...more...please?"

Cat covered Tamsin's hand with her other one, making her cousin's hand secure between hers. "The people there are all so happy. They love you so much that you can feel it even if they aren't hugging you or smiling at you. And you aren't lying in bed anymore. I saw you walking, running, and dancing."

Tamsin's eyes looked off into space. "I love... dance."

"There's a meadow and a playground and children who are sweet and kind. Oh, and there's a picnic, too."

Tamsin smiled at Cat. "Chili cheese fries?"

"Yes. Everything you like is there."

"Lovely," Tamsin said, staring up at her white ceiling.

"It is," Cat said. "It's a happy place, a safe place, and a place where you can do everything you used to do, or anything you've ever wanted to do."

"Ride... bike," Tamsin said, her eyes closing, leaving her delicate butterfly wing lashes resting on her cheeks.

"Up hills, down hills, even off jumps."

"Play Mousetrap... watch 'Dumbo'."

Cat noticed tears escaping from beneath her cousin's lashes. She leaned in and gave Tamsin a hug.

"Barrett?" Tamsin asked.

"He's still at the police station," Cat said. "I told them he didn't kidnap me, but they said they have to hold him for questioning. They told Aunt Marlow she could wait for him, but she said she'd go back and get him later."

"It won't be long now," Marlow called cheerfully as she entered the room. "The potatoes are boiling." Her voice slipped into anger. "What have you done?" Storming to the side of the bed, she grabbed Cat's arm. "You are not to make Tamsin cry."

"She didn't," Tamsin protested weakly, opening her eyes. "I… feel better."

"You don't have to cover for her, darling." Marlow pulled Cat to the door. "She needs to think about the consequences of her actions. When she comes back, she'll be better for you than ever."

Ignoring Tamsin's protest of, "No, Mother!" Marlow pulled Cat down the hall and yanked open the basement door. She pushed Cat through with enough force that Cat stumbled down several stairs until she lost her balance and fell against a stair hard enough to make a bruise. "You'd better think about what a nice place you have living here with us," Marlow said, her rigid body outlined at the top of the staircase. "When you start being grateful, then I'll think about letting you out." Then she shut the door. When Cat heard the lock turn, she crept up to the top step and leaned against the door, trembling in fear.

Chapter 24

Cat's stomach rumbled again. Folding her arms tightly across the hollow ache in her middle, she wondered what was being served in the Curious Circus mess tent. Everything she could imagine seemed wonderful.

Suddenly, a gentle wave of death rolled over her on its way somewhere. She straightened, thoughts of food darting from her mind as she tried to understand where death was headed. Was Tamsin dying now? Or was it Felicianna? Had something happened to Barry? Maybe the feeling rolled across the ocean from John Lamb. Had he suffered a fatal heart attack?

Cat clenched her hands together. For all she knew, it could even be Uncle Archie's last day on earth, his life snuffed out in a car accident. Or maybe she was going to die down here, forgotten in the basement.

Bumping her head against the door, she wondered why these feelings wouldn't just leave her alone. Head hurting, Cat wrapped her arms around her legs, lowered her head to her knees, and cried.

The sound of footfalls on the kitchen floor startled her from a restless doze. Cat sat up and wiped her eyes, hoping Marlow wouldn't be angry at her for crying.

When the footsteps passed the door, Cat sagged against it. How could Marlow know if Cat was being grateful if she kept ignoring her? It seemed as if Marlow was completely focused on Tamsin, to the point that she'd left Barry at the police station with officers who said they'd received an anonymous tip. The caller wasn't anonymous to Cat. Bendo had reported them, and the police weren't willing to believe her when she insisted that Barry hadn't kidnapped her.

They'd offered to wait for Marlow to get an attorney, but she'd given them a pained smile and asked them to call if Barry was ever released. Then she'd dragged Cat toward the exit.

As Cat glanced back at Barry, hoping to offer a small measure of comfort with her eye contact, she noticed the dark cloud lifting off his shoulders higher and higher as Marlow moved further away from him. By the time Marlow reached the door, Barry smiled at Cat from the brightness surrounding him. There was no darkness pressing in on him as he called, "See you later, alligator."

Cat waved just before Marlow pulled her out the door.

Chapter 25

The smell of pancakes seeped beneath the basement door, triggering fierce hunger. Either Tamsin had changed her mind about what she wanted to eat, or else she'd refused the potatoes and Marlow was trying something new to tempt her daughter into eating.

Cat imagined Marlow placing a stack of golden pancakes on a plate, melting butter in little golden pools on top before pouring glistening syrup down the sides. A glass of cold milk would go on the tray, and probably a fan of sliced strawberries to add a touch of cheerful color.

Cat would have been grateful for a handful of Circus Circles. She rubbed her arms and stared at the door, wondering how long it would be before she could get out of this cheerless basement.

Concentrating, she tried to envision what might happen if she knocked on the door. Would it irritate Marlow even more? Or would it remind her that Cat was still here, in case she'd forgotten?

Marlow's footsteps faded away, and Cat slumped against the door, feeling hopeless.

A few moments later, she heard a door open and heavy footsteps move across the kitchen floor. Those were not made by Marlow's feet.

"Hello?" she called.

The footfalls stopped for a tense moment. "Who's there?" Uncle Archie called.

"It's me, Cat," she answered, fighting back sudden tears. "I'm in the basement."

The feet hurried toward her. After some fumbling, the

door opened to let warm light flood in from the kitchen. "What are you doing in there?" Archie asked in amazement, putting his hand out to help Cat stand.

"I upset Aunt Marlow."

"You mean... she put you in there?" Archie's eyebrows shot up.

Cat nodded. "Tamsin was crying, but it was because she was happy. Aunt Marlow didn't believe me. She thought I'd hurt Tamsin's feelings."

"Oh, for the love..." Archie spun on his heel and bellowed, "Marlow!"

Cat slid around the wall away from Uncle Archie, desperate to distance herself from the tension in the room as Marlow approached the kitchen. "Oh, for goodness' sakes, keep your voice down," Marlow snapped as she came into view, wiping her hands on a dishtowel. Her eyes swept around the room and stopped on Cat.

Archie pointed at the basement door, each of his words coming out like a punch. "You locked her in the basement?"

Marlow's shoulders squared. "She had to be taught a lesson. It's not like I beat her or anything. I simply gave her a quiet place to think." Marlow headed for the stove and slung the dishtowel over the handle.

Archie followed her. "You can't possibly be in your right mind."

Marlow spun around. "Don't you dare say that to me."

"You're under a lot of stress."

Sensing that this conversation wasn't going anywhere good, Cat slid silently around the doorway into the front hall. As Archie and Marlow continued arguing, Cat opened the door and slipped outside.

She was free. She would run. Somehow she'd find a way to return to England.

Looking down the road one way and then the other, she tried to sense which was the best route to freedom. Should she go to the police station and look for Barry? If she could get him away from the station, they could change their names and find another circus to join, one that traveled to England. They wouldn't correct people who assumed they were brother and sister. They'd never talk about where they came from, and could say their birth certificates burned up or something.

Just as she turned left, a midnight blue Chevy Captiva pulled to a stop at the curb. Wishing she'd run sooner, Cat backed up. She wouldn't go back in the house, but she could run around to the back, climb the fence, and escape through a neighboring yard.

She tensed as the driver's door opened, then her mouth opened in shocked surprise as Officer Charlie Walters stepped out from behind the wheel. "Catriona!" he called, giving her a cheerful wave before hurrying around to the back of the car to pop the hatchback.

The passenger door opened and Barry slid out.

"You're back!" Cat cried, running forward to meet him in an embrace.

"Absolutely," Barry said, giving Catriona a solid hug. "He came and got me." Barry pointed at Charlie.

Quigley leapt out of the back of the car with a yelp and galloped toward Cat, who caught him in her arms and fell to the ground, tears of laughter running down her cheeks.

Charlie shut the hatchback. "Ellie wanted to come, but

she couldn't get off work. She sends her love."

"I can't believe you're here," Cat said. "I only just emailed John Lamb a couple of hours ago." She ruffled Quigley's ears. "Or maybe it was longer. I've been in the basement."

Charlie squatted down next to her and Barry copied him so that they sat like bookends on either side of Cat. "In the basement?" Charlie asked.

"It doesn't matter now," Cat said. "You're here, so everything's right again."

"I wasn't intentionally trying to deceive you," Charlie said. "It's just that things were in such a state that I never got 'round to telling you that I was the one emailing you from John Lamb's account, not until yesterday just before we left."

Cat straightened in surprise, and Quigley pulled free of her grasp to go for a sniff around the yard.

"It was you all along?"

"Yes. I hope that's all right. John asked me to take care of his work emails, so it's not like I was snooping. I just forgot to sign my name to my messages."

"So you...that explains how he knew about Quigley. He was you!" Then Cat's expression shifted to worry as she thought of the gentle wave of death that rolled over her in the basement. "So where is John Lamb? He's not... dead, is he?"

"Not last I saw him. He was going on holiday with his sister, and Ellie, Quigley and me were planning a road trip to see him after. But when I heard you'd gone missing, I came to find you. Well, we came." He glanced at Quigley. "I stopped at the station, and there was Barry, ready to come home."

A sudden sense of urgency rushed through Cat. She sprang to her feet. Grabbing Barry's hand, she said, "You need to go in and see Tamsin right now."

Barry followed willingly as Cat trotted toward the front door.

"What about me?" Charlie asked.

"Tamsin's allergic to dogs. You'd best stay out here with Quigley for a bit."

"Holler if you need me." Charlie put his hands in his pockets and watched Cat disappear into the house.

Ignoring Archie and Marlow arguing in the kitchen, Cat led the way down the hall to Tamsin's room. She pushed open the door to see Tamsin's eyes closed, her tray of pancakes untouched. Cat was wrong about the strawberry. Half a pink grapefruit glistened in a little white bowl, tilted to the side from the weight of a paring knife sticking out of it. Marlow must have been cutting it up for Tamsin when Archie called her to the kitchen.

"Tamsin?" Cat whispered.

Her cousin's big blue eyes fluttered open. As soon as they focused on Barry, Tamsin's lips turned up and she whispered, "Bear, you... came."

"Absolutely," Barry said. "Anything for you, Tam."

"Please... sit."

Barry headed for the chair next to Tamsin, but she said, "On... bed."

Barry sat and reached for his sister's hand. Instead of letting him take it, Tamsin lifted both of her thin arms a couple of inches off her mattress. Barry leaned down and carefully slid his hands around his sister's thin body, holding her in a gentle embrace.

"Ohhh," Tamsin sighed. "That's... better."

Barry rocked her gently back and forth. "If only you'd let me hug you before," he whispered while his tears dripped onto her pillow.

"I didn't know," Tamsin murmured. "It's...alright. I'm not...afraid now."

Barry's face pressed against his sister's hair. "But I don't want you to go."

"Bear." The nickname came out as soft as a sigh. "Going...good place. Always...love you." Then Tamsin relaxed. Barry held onto her for a moment longer, then carefully pulled his arms free.

"Is she...gone?" he asked, scanning his sister's still face.

Before Cat could reply, Marlow burst into the room. "What do you think you're doing?" she screamed. "No one is allowed in here but me! No one! Not even you! Not anymore!" She shoved Cat out of the way, then stumbled and fell against Barry, who caught her as he stood up from the bed. She pushed away from him and bent over Tamsin's still form.

"Tamsin, Mommy's here." Marlow smoothed her daughter's hair, but Tamsin lay perfectly still. Not even her thin chest moved with the slightest suggestion of breath. "Tamsin?" Marlow took hold of her daughter's shoulders and gave her a gentle shake. Tamsin's head rolled loosely around her pillow. "Tamsin!" Marlow screamed.

Her anguished gaze rose, landing on Cat. "You did this!" she wailed. "You killed her!" She lunged toward Cat, but Barry grabbed his cousin's shoulders and pulled her aside. Wild-eyed, Marlow spun and grabbed the knife from the grapefruit. Clutching it in her fist, she leapt toward Cat, jabbing at her with the blade.

Cat shrank back. Barry shoved her behind him, holding her with one hand while fending off his mother's attack with the other. "Ow!" Barry cried as the knife sunk into his skin.

"This is not your fight!" Marlow hissed.

"What is going on?" Archie yelled as he burst into the room.

"Take her," Barry called, letting go of Cat and reaching his uninjured hand out to yank the knife from his mother's hand.

Marlow stared at her son's bleeding wound, and then at the knife he gripped. Pressing her hands to her face, she collapsed to the floor, shaking with sobs.

Barry slowly knelt and tossed the knife across the floor. He reached out to embrace his mother, but as soon as she felt his touch, she jerked away and huddled into a miserable little ball on the floor.

"Are you alright?" Archie asked Cat.

Cat nodded, her eyes fixed on Barry and Marlow.

Archie took in a sharp breath, then stumbled over to his daughter's bed, staring at her lifeless body. He sank onto his daughter's mattress, took her body into his arms, and wept.

Cat caught Barry's eye, then handed him the napkin from Tamsin's food tray. Barry stood, wrapped the napkin around his hand, then sat beside his father and circled his arms around his shaking body. Archie's heartbreaking sobs calmed to soft crying within his son's embrace.

Cat bent down toward Marlow. Talking over her aunt's sobs, she said, "Now Tamsin is free to run, dance, sing, play, whatever she wants." Cat watched her aunt, unmoving, and thoughts of Linnea crept into her mind. Cat was separated from her own mother. Aunt Marlow had just lost a daughter.

Cat slid to her knees and wrapped her arms around Aunt Marlow.

Chapter 26

Cat gave Barry's uninjured hand an affectionate squeeze. Studying his face, she asked, "Are you going to be okay?"

"Better than okay. Dad said I could go back to work at the circus."

"What does Manny say?"

Barry looked puzzled. "He'll say yes, of course."

"I've already talked to him," Archie said, putting his arm across Barry's shoulder. "You're welcome to rejoin the circus right after your birthday. They're even planning to throw a welcome back party for you. How about if I come along and watch the show?"

"Absolutely! I'll introduce you to all my friends."

Archie thought a moment. "Is one of them named Gunther?"

"Yes. He's the strong man."

"Manny says he's changed since you were there."

Looking worried, Barry asked, "Is he all right?"

"It seems he wants to hug everyone, or at least pat them on the back." Archie demonstrated on Barry's back.

Barry relaxed. "Oh, he's okay, then. Any sort of touches done in kindness are healing. They're like mini hugs."

Cat looked up from where she sat beside Charlie. "Even a fist bump?" she asked with a grin.

Barry nodded. "Even that. It's better than no touch at all."

"But your touches seem to actually heal people," Archie said, his voice uncertain.

Barry grinned at him. "Everyone has different talents, Dad."

"Gunther had just better be careful not to squeeze anyone too hard," Charlie said.

Archie snapped his fingers as if he'd just remembered something. "Oh, yes, Manny told me that horseback rider doesn't have a broken back after all. She's just bruised, and she'll be back at the circus next week, just in time for them to move on to Pennsylvania."

Barry nodded. "I knew she'd be all right as soon as I hugged her."

"Could you have healed Tamsin?" Archie asked quietly. "I mean, if she had let you, you know? Hug her."

Barry's face grew solemn. "I don't know, Dad. Everyone dies sometime. But even if hugs wouldn't have healed her, they would have made her feel so much better."

Archie gave his son's shoulders a squeeze, then glanced at the clock. "I need to go. It's time for me to visit your mother."

"Can I come with you?" Barry asked.

"I don't know if you'll like it."

"Why?"

"She's in a mental hospital."

"Does Mother like it there?"

Archie sighed. "I don't know. She's not talking to anyone."

"I'd like to come and give her a hug."

"I don't know if she wants one."

"Then I'll just keep visiting her until she does."

Archie gave Barry a soft smile. "I'm glad you're my son."

"Me, too, Dad." Barry stuck out his fist, and his father touched his knuckles with a fist of his own. Then he pulled Barry into a hug.

"Time for us to go, too," Charlie said.

"Just a minute," Cat said. Pulling out her colorful hat, she handed it to Barry. "Take a bit of my with you on your circus adventures."

"I'd rather it was really you," Barry said, looking steadily into Cat's eyes.

Cat stared back, then said, "I'll see you again, Barry. This is just goodbye for now."

Barry hugged Cat, then Charlie, then Quigley. "If the Curious Circus comes to England, come and see me again," Barry said. "Quigley can come, too, and make friends with Seal Dog."

"Great idea," Charlie said.

Archie gave Cat a hug and shook Charlie's hand, then he and Barry got in their car and drove off in the direction of the hospital. Barry waved the colorful hat out the window, the tiny jingle bells bouncing on their short fringes until the car drove out of sight.

Charlie turned to Cat. "Are you ready to go home?"

"Do I really get to live with you and Ellie?"

"If you're willing. We would like nothing better than to have you and Quigley in our home. Is that alright with you?"

Cat grinned, grabbed Quigley's leash, and headed for the car. "Absolutely."

THE END

Please feel free to check out Merrill's fascinating first book written with Bahlmann, which he describes as a novelized version of his life: Faith, Hope, and Gravity

Biographies

Merrill Davis Osmond was born the middle child of George and Olive Osmond. The lead singer of the famous Osmonds, he is also a songwriter and producer. Merrill sang lead to the group's collective unbelievable 27 gold records - many of which he shared the production credits and has written the music and lyrics for five number one hit records. Collectively, the Osmonds have produced 47 platinum and gold records, and his entertainment career has spanned over 54 years. Merrill produced over 90 teleplays and scripts, which include "The Donny & Marie Show" on ABC (1976-1979), "The Roy Clark Special," "The Osmond Family Christmas Special" and many others. Two Presidents have requested his expertise in producing two prominent events, "The Making of an Inauguration" for President Ronald Reagan, and on behalf of President George Bush's Inauguration in 1989, "The Quincentennial Inaugural Ball."

Merrill, co-founder of the "Osmond Foundation," now known as the "Children's Miracle Network," is currently involved in moving forward his late mother's dream of assisting those with hearing loss through the Olive Osmond Hearing Fund.

Merrill is also an author of two previous books, "Let the Reason be Love" a memoir of his life and "The Plan Revisited" which tells the journey of writing a life changing album "The Plan."

Merrill and wife, Mary, have six children & 15 grandchildren. Visit his website at:
www.merrillosmond.com
Facebook:
https://www.facebook.com/merrilldavisosmond
Twitter:
http://twitter.com/#!/merrillosmond

Shirley Anderson Bahlmann has written a wide variety of genres, including historical fiction, novels, biographies, how-to, and how-not-to books. Shirley finds the most annoying thing about being a prolific writer is the need to sleep, because she'd rather be writing.

You are welcome to visit her website:
http://shirleybahlmann.com/

Blog: http://shirleybahlmann.blogspot.com/

Or if you like to tweet, she's here, too:
http://twitter.com/#!/shirleybahlmann

Be her friend on Facebook (because everyone needs friends!)
https://www.facebook.com/shirleybahlmann

ACKNOWLEDGEMENTS:

Thanks to Shirley Ann Hales for her eagerness to read the story, a motivating factor in getting it completed!

Catrina Mary Walters was invaluable in helping answer questions about places and things related to the United Kingdom that might be different than the way things are done or referred to in America.

Many thanks to the invaluable proofreaders Linda G. Pratt, Janet Olsen, and Mary Kay Olsen.

Cover photos by Professor Andrew Robert Bahlmann.
Cover models: Marcus Bahlmann and Anneke Bahlmann.

www.ingramcontent.com/pod-product-compliance
Lightning Source LLC
Chambersburg PA
CBHW071258130626
46556CB00003B/1363